Twelve Trees

OTHER BOOKS BY J. D. CARPENTER

POETRY
Nightfall, Ferryland Head
Swimming at Twelve Mile
Lakeview
Compassionate Travel

FICTION
The Devil in Me
Bright's Kill
74 Miles Away

J.D. CARPENTER

Twelve Trees

A Novel

THE DUNDURN GROUP
TORONTO

Editor: Barry Jowett
Copy-editor: Shannon Whibbs
Designer: Erin Mallory
Printer: Marquis

Library and Archives Canada Cataloguing in Publication

Carpenter, J.D.
    Twelve trees / J.D. Carpenter.

ISBN 978-1-55002-798-3

    I. Title.

PS8555.A7616T94 2008   C813'.54   C2008-900391-8

1 2 3 4 5   12 11 10 09 08

Conseil des Arts
du Canada

Canada Council
for the Arts

Canada

ONTARIO ARTS COUNCIL
CONSEIL DES ARTS DE L'ONTARIO

We acknowledge the support of the **Canada Council for the Arts** and the **Ontario Arts Council** for our publishing program. We also acknowledge the financial support of the **Government of Canada** through the **Book Publishing Industry Development Program** and **The Association for the Export of Canadian Books**, and the **Government of Ontario** through the **Ontario Book Publishers Tax Credit program** and the **Ontario Media Development Corporation**.

Care has been taken to trace the ownership of copyright material used in this book. The author and the publisher welcome any information enabling them to rectify any references or credits in subsequent editions.

J. Kirk Howard, President

Printed and bound in Canada
www.dundurn.com

Dundurn Press	Gazelle Book Services Limited	Dundurn Press
3 Church Street, Suite 500	White Cross Mills	2250 Military Road
Toronto, Ontario, Canada	High Town, Lancaster, England	Tonawanda, NY
M5E 1M2	LA1 4XS	U.S.A. 14150

for Lawrence Scanlan

ACKNOWLEDGEMENTS

Ulrike Bender, Joe Broughton, Hadley Carpenter, Peter Carpenter, Warner Clarke, Brian L. Flack, Beth Hoen, Barry Jowett, D'Arcy Lynn, Selby Martin, John McKinney, Matthew Murphy, Stephen Murphy, Karen Ralley, Rick Short, Cathy Stanfield, Susan Straiton, George Valliere, Kathy Varley

Mourn as you may for your brave son, you will take nothing by it. You cannot raise him from the dead, ere you do so yet another sorrow shall befall you.

— Achilles to Priam, *The Iliad*, Book XXIV

FIRST RACE

(7 Furlongs.
3-Year-Olds and Up.
Claiming $10,000.
Purse $15,500.)

1 Shawna's Hope
2 Our Pet
3 Harpsichord
4 Tell Joe
5 Impending
6 Outskirts
7 Around the Horn
8 Kinship
9 What It Is
10 Little Ruckus
11 Burglar

Someone climbs on the stool to my right. I lift my eyes from the *Racing Form*, but I don't recognize the guy. Small and wiry. Nasty scar on his cheek, like a pucker. Bullet, maybe, or maybe he had a cyst removed. When Dexter walks up and says, "What'll it be?" the man says, "Large draft and, let's see, a Tequila Sunrise." He drops a ten-dollar bill on the bar. Dexter picks up the money, gives the man his steady, unamused look and says, "I'll get you the beer, but it could be you've had too much tequila already."

"Fine, whatever," the man says and waves Dexter away. He turns to me and says, "Why's it so hard to get a drink around here? They gave me a hard time at the Swan, too."

I glance at the Blue Light clock behind the bar. "It's twenty past noon," I say. "Maybe Dexter's got rules about how deep into the day he can serve a Sunrise."

The man narrows his eyes. "Is that a joke? Are you trying to be funny?"

I shake my head. "Not at all. You asked a question, I answered it."

The man looks me up and down. "What the hell kind of suit is that?"

"It's called a plantation suit."

The man shakes his head just like I did. "I'm not going to argue with you," he says. "I won't argue with you."

Dexter returns and puts the beer and the change from the ten dollars in front of the man.

As he pockets the change the man says, "You've been inside, haven't you, pal."

Dexter looks at him. "No, I've never been inside."

"Oh yes, you have. I know you. I was inside, too. I remember you."

"You must be thinking of someone else," Dexter says evenly. "I've never been inside in my life."

The man nods his head emphatically. "Oh, yes, you have. I remember you. Worked in the laundry."

"Who did? I did?"

"We both did."

"What's your name?"

The man laughs. "They called me Short Eyes inside, but my friends call me Billy."

Dexter frowns. "I'm pretty good with faces, but I don't remember ever seeing you before."

"You calling me a liar?"

Dexter takes a breath and says, "Take it easy —"

"Are you? I just want to know. I don't want to argue with you, but I want to know if that's what you're doing. Calling me a liar."

Dexter lowers his chin. "You'd better behave, mister, or I'm gonna have to ask you to leave."

The man smiles, shakes his head, and waves his hand at Dexter again. "I'm all behaved out," he says.

Dexter goes to the cash register at the far end of the bar and opens the drawer. He walks back and drops a ten in front of the man. "There's your money back. Now get out." He takes away the man's beer.

"What the hell," says the man. "I paid for that beer, I'll damn well drink it."

Dexter leans to his left and pours the man's beer into the bar sink, strides away from us — past the tiny carwash the dirty glasses pass through, under the Lucky Draw Muskoka Chair hanging from the ceiling — takes something from under the bar, makes his turn at the cash register where Jessy's punching in an order with one hand and straightening her hair with the other, and starts down our side of the bar. Dexter's not a tall man, he's not heavy either, but you can see the power in his shoulders. Plus, even though it's November, he's wearing shorts, those Lycra cycling shorts, black ones, and you can see the muscles in his legs. As well, he's smacking the business end of a black walking stick against the palm of his hand.

11

"Motherfucker," the man says, scrambling off his stool. "You black motherfucker," he says, and beetles out the door.

Dexter walks back down to the end of the bar, makes his turn — Jessy hasn't noticed a thing — tosses the walking stick under the bar, comes along to where I'm sitting, scoops up the ten and drops it in the tips bowl beside the jar of pickled eggs.

I return to my reading. I narrow it down to Outskirts and Little Ruckus. I look up at the bank of televisions mounted to the wall above the tiers of liquor bottles. A hockey player is being interviewed on TV #4, farthest to my right. On TV #3 a bronzed young woman in a bikini is dancercising on a tropical beach. TV #2 is asking the question WHICH AMERICAN PRESIDENT WAS ASSASSINATED BY LEON CZOLGOSZ IN THE TEMPLE OF MUSIC? And printed in bold white figures against a cerulean background on TV #1 are the track odds for the first race at Caledonia Downs. Outskirts is 6-1; Little Ruckus is 9-5. But Little Ruckus is a son of Bold Ruckus, a speed sire, and I remember his dam, Little Wonder, who ran around here a few years ago. Cheap sprinter who usually ran out of gas after five furlongs. We're going seven here, and even though he's the chalk I don't think Little Ruckus can get the distance.

I get off my bar stool. I leave my glasses on top of the *Form* and walk over to where Dale is standing by the railing that separates the dance floor and the pool table from the booths.

"My man," Dale says.

"Greetings," I reply and place three five-dollar bills on his tray. "Five across on the six, please."

Dale writes down the information on his clipboard. "Five across on number six. Duly noted." When you place a bet with Dale he always repeats it for you so there'll be no misunderstandings later. The guy at the video store does the same thing. "*Shrek*," he'll say, before slipping the videotape into a plastic box for you. Or, in my case, "*Naughty Nymphos*," or whatever alluring title I've selected from the shelves of the little room behind the swinging, saloon-style doors.

Back at the bar I put my glasses on and raise my eyes to TV #1: the yellow-shirted members of the starting crew are loading the horses into the gate.

Both Outskirts and Little Ruckus break alertly. For the first three furlongs they run like a matched team. At the half-mile pole my horse is a head in front. At the top of the stretch, Little Ruckus quits, just like his mother would have done, but a longshot, Burglar, rushes up on the outside. Halfway down the lane the three-horse makes a charge as well, but neither of them can get by me, and after what is a truly thrilling stretch run — a kind of low-end version of Easy Goer and Sunday Silence, or Affirmed and Alydar, during which I become aware of the profound thumping of my heart and a desire to mount the bar and scream at the TV but manage to limit myself to a kind of croaking "Come on six, come on you *six*!" combined with a rhythmic nodding of my head in sync with the thrusting action of the jockey as he pushes the horse's neck with one hand and whacks its hindquarters with the whip in his other; all around me the growing clamour of my bar-mates and fellow gamblers, most of whom have at least a few dollars and some of whom have many dollars riding on the race, money even now sprouting wings in Dale's pockets unless it has Outskirts' name attached to it — Outskirts crosses the finish line a valiant neck to the good.

"Yes!" I exclaim and clap my hands and beam around

at the general confusion — the air full of cigarette smoke and Garth Brooks and four-letter words and whoops and grunts and yelps. I turn to Old Gordon, sitting on the stool to my left staring into his rye and ginger, and I sing, "I'm gonna moo-oove, way on the outskirts of town!" but he just looks at me with a startled expression on his face, as if I'd wakened him — which, indeed, I might have.

I'm particularly pleased because if Outskirts had lost, I'd be in trouble. The fifteen dollars I bet was not my money. It represents three-tenths of a fifty-dollar bill I "borrowed" from a lady friend named Anna, who foolishly left her purse in my care while she made the rounds at Vesuvio's last night (dinner was her treat, it goes without saying). Times are tough, and I have to count every penny. Here at McCully's, the stalwart Dexter's been a big help. Unlike the barkeeps at the other bars I patronize, who are stingy when it comes to granting a man a little credit, Dexter lets me run a monthly tab.

When the numbers come up I quickly jot them down. It's $14.50 to win, $6.30 to place, $4.70 to show. Two and a half times each grosses me $63.75, less the $15 I bet, less a deuce for Dale.

I like to hit early. It's the only way to start the day. Even when I'm flush, I'll stop betting if I lose the first couple of races. I'll keep on watching and making notes, but I won't bet. Call me superstitious, but I'll feel like I just don't have the touch that particular day, that the stars aren't properly aligned. If I lose the first couple of races, I lose my confidence, and you can't beat the ponies if you don't think you can.

And, unlike the old days when I'd kick myself in hindsight for not betting more on a horse that won, or for neglecting to play the Daily Double — which is, in fact, what I've just done now — I don't worry about it. I just nod to Dexter, and he brings me another pint.

I'm just completing my calculations when the door to the street opens and Mrs. Belyea steps from the sunshine into the gloom. It takes a moment for her eyes to adjust to the darkness in the bar, but as soon as she sees me, she makes a beeline.

"Mr. Harvey, Mr. Harvey!" she exclaims. "I'm sorry to bother you, Mr. Harvey, but have you seen my Tommy? He didn't come home for lunch and I'm worried sick."

Mrs. Belyea is dressed in a scarlet jogging outfit, white socks, and orthopedic sandals. Her bleached blonde hair is dishevelled, her lips are smeared with bright red lipstick, and she's smoking a menthol cigarette about a foot long.

The problem with Mrs. Belyea is she's crazy as a squirrel. She thinks her son is twelve years old. In fact, Tommy's a grown man. But at least once a day I hear from her. Because she and Tommy share an apartment on the same floor of the Everdon Arms as I do, she considers me a neighbour and friend. So, at least once a day I get a phone call: "Sorry to bother you, Mr. Harvey, but by any chance would my Tommy be there? I just can't find that boy anywhere." "No, Mrs. Belyea," I'll say, as I lower the volume or put down the sandwich out of which I was about to take my first bite, "I haven't seen him all day. He's probably at work." "Oh no, Mr. Harvey, not Tommy, he's only twelve years old! I've just phoned John, and he's coming straight home to help me look." John, her husband, has been dead a decade. "I've got his dinner on the table, but I just can't think where he might be. Off playing with his friends, I suppose." Tommy, who is tall, pale, and unhappy-looking, has — to my knowledge, at least — no friends. I suspect he considers *me* a friend, which just goes to show how unfortunate he is. Nervous and distractible, he shambles and hangs his head when he walks and always seems to have about two days' growth on his chin. The only thing he seems interested in is his mother, but I get the impression that he doesn't love her so much as he's shackled to her. He occasionally wanders down the hall to my place to get away from her, and, during one such visit, just last week, he told me she's recently taken to setting four places at the table — one for herself, one for her late husband, one for Tommy, and one for Tommy's phantom brother. Tommy is an only child, which makes me wonder whether she isn't, in her addledness, resurrecting some long-hid secret — an abortion, perhaps, or a child born out of wedlock and put up for adoption before she met Mr. Belyea. I've never mentioned these possibilities to Tommy, who's got problems enough of his own — finding a girlfriend being number one, finding a decent job number two. Currently he's working in customer inquiries, which means he's one of many customer inquirers sitting at a profusion of telephones in an office building somewhere, phoning people at home, usually at suppertime, asking if they'd be interested in subscribing to a certain magazine or a certain concert series, or selling their house, or feeding the children, or putting bags of used clothing on their porch for pick-up, or having their attic insulated, or their chimney cleaned. Last month, Tommy was a busboy at a Greek restaurant on the Danforth, and the month before that he was "consulting," whatever that meant.

So here, now, in the bar, I say, "Tommy's twenty-three years old, Mrs. Belyea. He's at work. He works from noon till eight. He'll be home at eight-thirty."

Mrs. Belyea gives me an indulgent laugh. "No, no, Mr.

Harvey, you must be thinking of my older boy. He likes to be called Tommy, too!"

Recently, Mrs. Belyea has gotten into the habit of knocking on my door looking for Tommy. And just last week she came right in without knocking. It must have been about eleven in the morning because I was sitting on the pullout couch watching *The View*, and I mustn't have heard her come in because when I turned and saw her standing in the hall closet I went about four feet in the air. "Good Christ, Mrs. Belyea!" I said. She turned and looked at me and said, "I'm looking for Tommy. Have you seen him?" "He's not here," I said, shaking. My words had no effect; she continued to poke her nose between the clothes hangers. "I can't find that boy anywhere," she said. I sat back down on the couch and leaned over and poured myself a Bushmills to settle my nerves and when I turned back around, she was gone. Ten minutes later I had to take a leak, so I walked down the hall and there she was in my bathroom smoking a cigarette. "Mrs. Belyea," I said, "what are you doing?" She looked at me sort of befuddled for a few seconds, then collected herself and said, "Sorry to bother you, Mr. Harvey, but have you seen my Tommy?"

I look at Dexter and he gives me a little lift of the head. He doesn't want her here. That's another problem with Mrs. Belyea: booze and her don't get along. She likes her cocktails, and after a couple or three Singapore Slings she'll come on to whoever's sitting on the stool next to her, quite often men only half her age, young men who find her ridiculous and either insult her or take her outside and into the alley behind the bar, or out between the Dumpsters behind the Price Chopper, where they have their fun with her, and she comes back fifteen minutes later rumpled and confused. We never see the young men again; they find other places to drink.

"He's not here, Mrs. Belyea."

She takes a ladylike drag on her cigarette and blows the smoke skyward. "Thank you so much," she says. "I'm sorry to have bothered you." Then she makes her slow, unsteady, stately way back out to the street, where, before the door eases shut behind her, I can hear her calling out, "Tommy! *Tommy!*"

Today is a special day. It was one year ago exactly that two calamities befell me within a few hours of each other: my employer, *Sport of Kings* Magazine, fired me — for the final time — and Barbara left me.

Barbara is a real estate agent, and a damned good one. I'd been dry for several months and we were renting a three-bedroom brick detached in the new Babbling Brook development when, one night at dinner, she started talking about buying a time-share condo somewhere in Muskoka, a second Belgian shepherd to be a companion for the one she already had, a second Saturn to match the one she already had, and getting married. I got up from the table, grabbed my jacket, drove down here to McCully's, fell off the wagon in spectacular style, failed to report for work the next morning, and by that evening found myself unemployed and single. That was a year ago today, November 10, 2003. A Monday. Not a good way to start the week.

Nowadays I drink even more than I used to. In fact, with the exception of gambling, my life is pretty much devoted to drinking. But without Barbara around to nag me, and without my job making impositions on my time, drinking isn't a problem anymore. I can drink all day long if I want to, and no one gives me a hard time, least of all my cronies here at the bar who, to a greater or lesser degree, are drunks themselves. Even Mrs. Belyea wound up at the Everdon Arms because of her drinking. The Everdon's basically a rooming house for alcoholics, but because her brain's gone soft on her, not only does she think her husband's still alive and Tommy's still twelve, she thinks she still lives in the suburbs. Last week she invited me to a pool party at her house. "Forest Trailway," she told me. "Number eleven. Just walk right around to the back. Don't forget your trunks and a patio chair. And whatever you do, don't be late, or you'll miss out on John's famous margaritas."

In the old life my job encouraged drinking. Or you could say drinking went with the job: journalism — of the racetrack variety. Articles on rich owners, their brittle-coiffed wives, dishonest trainers, and smart-assed jockeys. Or on the true athletes — the horses themselves, the only players in the game who didn't offer me money for a favourable piece.

Towards the end of my tenure at *Sport of Kings* I would wake up rocky from the previous night's drinking and, trying not to wake Barbara, would stumble around in the dark looking for my underpants. Halfway through the workday I would notice — when I was on the crapper, more than likely — that I was wearing one blue sock and one brown. On one occasion I was on the subway to work, standing in the crush of commuters, doing my best not to go flying every time the subway stopped or started or entered or exited a curve, when I noticed a small group of teenagers — seated, of course — leaning together and tittering and pointing at my feet. I looked down. My socks were the same colour, but I was wearing a Wallabee on my left foot and a brogue on my right.

One of the reasons I loved being a racetrack journalist was because I was a gambler, too. I'd bet on anything — horses, cards, slots, dogs, baseball, basketball, football, hockey, soccer. I'd bet you the next person who walked by would be a woman. Give me odds, and I'd bet on the colour of her hair. I'd bet you the next vehicle to go by would be an SUV. Give me odds, and I'd bet on the make. If you liked baseball, I'd bet you how many walks would be issued in a certain game, how many home runs hit, how many double plays turned, how many errors committed.

One time, I bet heavily on a filly called Coral Island. She was running second in a tiny field of four, but she was so far behind the leader by the midway point of the stretch that I'd given up all hope, and that's when the leader, Flag of Victory, who was out front all by herself, snapped a foreleg and fell. The jockey was thrown hard, and the filly rolled on top of him. Suddenly the people rooting for Flag of Victory fell silent, and I started yelling, "Go four! Go, you four!" Coral Island ended up the winner, and when I turned away from the screen — this was at the off-track, and I was jumping up and down only inches away from that huge screen they have there — still pumping my fist in celebration at this uncommon good luck, I realized I was the only one making any noise at all, and all these people were glaring at me like I was a baby killer. And that was when I was at my worst — gambling-wise anyway — when I sank so low that I didn't even care about the tragedy that had just taken place on the track — a jockey lying motionless in the dirt; a filly squealing in pain and terror and trying to right herself, her left foreleg shattered and dangling below the knee. All I cared about was the wager.

Because I couldn't stop betting, I lost a lot of money. And as a result of losing a lot of money, I did a lot of drinking, and as a result of both I lost my girlfriend and my job. I remember Barbara standing at the front door of the house we were renting, her suitcases at her feet. Outside, a taxi was idling. I was leaning against the banister with a drink in my hand. We had the house till the end of the month — another three weeks — so I was in no hurry to go anywhere. Barbara could have stayed, too, but she'd had enough: "You're basically a good man, Priam," she told me. "And I know you love me. But you love gambling more, and you love drinking more than you love gambling, and I'm not going to play *third* fiddle — let alone second fiddle — to your bad habits. It's such a shame," she said, "such a waste."

I never got her back, of course. She was too smart for that. When she walked out the door and got into the taxi, that was the last time I saw her.

"Dexter."

"Yes, Mr. Harvey."

"A pint, please."

I study horse racing, make a science of it. I bet a lot of races, but I don't bet a lot of money. Not anymore. Still, most afternoons you'll find me right here at McCully's Tavern, subsidizing Dale's retirement fund. What with Barbara gone and my career just another tragic chapter in the history books, I'm easy to find. I'm with the bookies and barflies and reprobates. I'm with the hustlers and rummies and all the other desperate characters sliding helplessly down the greased pole of life.

McCully's is just a neighbourhood bar where, as it happens, you can place a bet with one of the bookies — Dale or

Consensus or Ringo — who operate out of here on an entirely unpredictable basis. There is no real McCully, so far as I know. That's just a clever idea from the friendly folks at Hearth&Home, who own the rundown hotel that sits on top of McCully's like a chicken on an egg. It's like one of those bar names you hear a lot of these days — names like Jawny Baker's or Paddy O'Farrell's — that are supposed to give the impression that the place is old and established, and that it's actually owned and operated by somebody by that name, and if you're real lucky he might even be there at the bar when you go in, buying a round for the house. Before Hearth&Home bought the building, it was the Grove Hotel, and the habitués of its bar called it the Grove, as in "If anybody's looking for me, I'll be at the Grove." I've been drinking here, off and on, for over twenty years. Whatever its name, this bar's always been a haven for me.

After you've made your bet, you can watch the race on TV #1, which illegally beams in the Jockey Club telecast. Everyone in here is quite happy to rip the Jockey Club off of their 20 percent or whatever it is of every dollar bet. We'd much rather see Consensus or Dale or Ringo pocket the profit than those rich bastards who are responsible for closing all the small local tracks, including Dundas Park, which until last year was right across the street from McCully's, right here *inside* the city, not out in the monster-home suburbs. Real thoroughbred racing every spring and fall; harness racing every summer and winter. But the fat cats at the Jockey Club closed it down and sold it for a townhouse development, and reduced us — the horsemen — to watching horse racing on TV, something I never thought I would lower myself to. Half the people who drink at McCully's are out-of-work racetrackers — hotwalkers and grooms and parimutuel clerks and exercise boys. Now, instead of making their living at Dundas Park, they sit in here and drink. But the fat cats don't care. It's the siege mentality. Them or us. It's the class struggle, plain and simple. Rich getting richer, poor poorer. And to think I used to hobnob with them, attend their parties, rub shoulders with them — the fat bastards, their brittle-coiffed wives. I used to send them up. All those years I had myself tricked into thinking I was a hard-nosed reporter earning an honest buck I was really nothing but a lackey. I was nothing but a bootlicker to them.

Now there's just one racetrack, Caledonia Downs, thirty miles from here, out where the fat cats live. And because it's pretty much impossible to get to — what with traffic gridlock and not being able to afford a car anyway — a lot of us have quit going to the track and are sitting on our butts at home, betting the races by phone or Internet, and watching the races on our computers or TVs, losing our money in the comfort of our own apartments or furnished rooms or hovels or Dumpsters or whatever we happen to be living in. The worst part about playing the horses at home is that you're alone. In the old days, at least you could blow your wad in the company of friends and fellow racetrackers. That's why I come to McCully's. If I stayed home, I'd be in a kind of solitary confinement, with nothing to do except phone my money in to the betting channel. What with that and the shopping channel and phone sex and playing poker on the Internet, I'd never have to go outside at all.

Dexter places my beer in front of me.

"Thank you, Dexter."

"Welcome."

The other day I had nothing much to do so I did some calculating: at a rate of ten races per day, two hundred days per year, and thirty-five years, I figure I've watched — live or on TV, thoroughbred and standardbred — close to seventy thousand horse races in my life.

I've watched so many races that I can tell when a horse in the middle of the pack is starting to lag by the way his head begins to bob or his tail begins to swish. I've even detected the hitch in a horse's action that indicates he's broken something, and on more than one occasion I've waited breathlessly to see what would happen next. Would the horse go down, and would the followers tumble over him, or would he struggle bravely on, like Cool Reception in the '67 Belmont, running on the stump?

I like both kinds of racing, thoroughbred and standardbred. Despite their lower social status, I like betting the trots just as much as I do the flats. The jughead is the common man's horse, the blue collar horse. Thoroughbreds are owned by millionaires; standardbreds are owned by farmers and cabbies and posties and pensioners. Even though I hung out with high society the last few years I was with the magazine, in my heart I've always identified with the jugheads. Homely and nondescript and middle-class. Me to a T.

And even though the jockey on a thoroughbred has more room to move, and less difficulty maneuvering his mount through traffic and past tired horses, the standardbred driver in his buggy has a different kind of dexterity, and the way the horses string out single file along the rail — until the backstretch when the trailers tip out from cover and then spread out across the track at the head of the stretch for the final charge to the wire — excites me so much that sometimes when I'm walking home along Queen Street after an evening of betting and watching the trots, I imagine myself in a sulky behind a jughead, whip in hand, and, after using the cover of some unsuspecting pedestrian ahead of me, I'll tip out and scoot past him just before we pass the red mailbox or the front door of the Swan or whatever it is that I've marked as the finish line.

No, I think horses are beautiful and I think horse racing is beautiful, but I must admit a big part of the attraction is the gambling. I've won eighty thousand dollars in a single afternoon and, once, a long time ago, I lost fifty thousand in thirty minutes at a high roller baccarat table in Las Vegas.

But like I say, I don't bet big anymore. I'll still make the occasional exotic bet. A few years ago, for example, I bet Consensus two hundred dollars even-up that Rick's Natural Star would finish last in the Breeder's Cup mile. Last? I don't think he even finished the race. I think he's still running. That bet was a lock.

Adrenalin. That's why I do it. It's a nervous life — just ask Barbara, if you can find her — but I was happier on the edge, risking everything, than I ever could have been teaching school or selling insurance or scraping the plaque off people's teeth. It was the rush I got. It was my dope. At one time I would rather gamble than do anything — drink, write, chase women, you name it.

Now, I would just as soon drink.

I arrive at the bar with great singularity of purpose: I nod to the barman — depending on where I am, the barman will acknowledge me by name, or simply nod and say, "What'll it be?" If it's McCully's, Dexter will place a pint of Creemore in front of me without my having to say a word, and Jessy will stop by my stool at some point during the proceedings to ask me if I want something to eat. I have to admit I like being known. Like at Five Star Barbers, for example. They call me The Professor, and I know their names — Joe and Mario and Lenny — and I always ask after their wives and children, and I never have to tell them what kind of cut I want.

I drink at McCully's or the Linsmore or the Black Swan or Terri O's or The Willow or The Diamond.

I didn't always drink in places like this. When Barbara left, I hung around jazz bars. I liked the anonymity. I could sit alone at a table, and nobody knew me from Adam. For years I'd dreamed of doing nothing except hang around jazz bars, and here at last was my opportunity. I sought out the real jazz players, the few that were still alive and happened to be passing through town. I saw Sonny Rollins and Ornette Coleman and Wayne Shorter and Joe Lovano and Joe Henderson. I saw Keith Jarrett and Herbie Hancock and the Brecker Brothers and Lester Bowie. I had a good time for a while, but two things ended up ruining it: this jazz I was listening to turned out to be bad for me — the ballads they played conjured up broken love affairs and regret, and their fast tunes made me frantic. As well, the women I met at these bars were even more desperate than I was, sitting at tables close to the bandstand, bobbing their heads in time to the music, chain-smoking. And the two or three relationships that developed during that sad period of my life went nowhere. They were trashy and short-lived. What I needed was a place where I could drink *happily*. After what I'd been through — losing Barbara and my job, pretty much all my self-esteem, and something I don't talk about much, which was the murder, three years ago, of my son — I had good reason to drink. I had no reason not to drink. But I wanted to drink happy. So, no more jazz bars for me.

So one day about three years ago I'm walking along

Queen Street, and I happen to look in through the windows of McCully's, which I hadn't visited since it was the Grove, and my eyes catch sight of the unmistakable blue of a track-odds TV screen. It's a bright sky-blue — a hopeful blue. I ask myself what would a track-odds TV be doing in a bar in a Hearth&Home Hotel, so in I go to find out. There's this tall skinny guy with a laptop standing at the island. "I see that TV has track odds on it," I say to him, jerking my thumb at what I later learn is TV #1. "Can people make bets in here?" He says, "Are you a cop?" I laugh, and I guess he can tell I'm not because right away he says, "You can bet with me." It turns out this was Consensus I was talking to. And that's how I ended up here — where hope lives, where every twenty minutes I can buy another small fix from one of the dealers. The *hope* dealers. As little as a buck a bet, as much as two hundred. Every twenty minutes — all afternoon and all evening if I want to — I can buy hope.

I never sit at a table. I always sit at the bar with my feet on the brass rail and my elbows on the polished wood, my forearms forming a tepee, a cigarette sending smoke signals from my fingers. If I'm here at McCully's to watch the races and make a few bets, the cigarette pack and its lead-pony book of matches stay on the bar beside my *Form*, and, once settled, I'm likely to stay here all afternoon and, if there's an evening card of harness racing at Mohawk, I might still be here at ten at night. I'll drink a dozen pints and half a dozen shots and smoke a pack of Player's Light, and then I'll hum myself back to the Everdon and lay my weary body down.

Sometimes, I must admit, my life seems pretty sad. Fifty-six years old, no job, nothing but a crummy apartment to call home. No wife or kids. No friends — except a burned-out ex-cop named Campbell Young and the rest of the motley crew of drinkers whose company I keep, some of whose lives are even sadder than my own. But I try to be philosophical about it. Which means, whenever I start getting depressed I have a couple of drinks and in a little while I don't feel so bad. To tell the truth, I'm not unhappy. I look at it this way: it used to be true that all I could think about were the things I didn't have. Money. Prestige. Family. Time. I was resentful about the things I didn't have and the things I could no longer do — simple things, like climb a flight of stairs without panting like a bastard at the top. Nowadays, however, what with so many people having strokes or getting cancer or being downsized or dying in terrorist attacks or earthquakes or being ethnically cleansed, I'm happy about the things I *do* have. A sound heart. Relative sanity. A few bucks in my pocket. And time. Bags and bags of time. Some mornings I won't get out of bed till noon. Some days the first thing I do is have a drink. Then I'll fry up a whole pound of bacon, or if I don't want to smell up my kitchen or I don't feel like cooking, I'll walk down to Ginger's and have the all-day breakfast.

What it boils down to is I do what I want. I'll go a week without shaving. I'll wear the same shirt five days running. If I owned a car, and if it was a blisteringly hot day in August, I'd drive with the air conditioning on *and* the windows open.

Dale gives me sixty-four dollars. He likes to round off. I put two dollars on his tray.

"Much obliged," he says. He smiles. Dale's got this shy smile and a sort of courtly way of talking. He's not your typical bookie. Consensus is tall and skinny and looks like an ostrich; Ringo's tall and skinny and looks like a vulture.

And where Consensus is kind of wary and Ringo's kind of surly, Dale, who's medium height and roly-poly and looks like a friendly plumber, is polite and sympathetic and will buy you a drink if you're on a losing streak. "Too bad you didn't bet the Double," he says.

"Anybody selling?" Sometimes people who win the first half of the Daily Double but decide they don't like the chances of their horse in the second will sell their ticket, if they're offered the right price.

"The twins might be willing."

The twins dress like country-clubbers in cardigans and sports coats, but are in fact common or garden-variety alcoholics who almost always lose. Ronny, the more talkative of the two, often wins early when he's still relatively sober, but by the end of the day he's trying to borrow money off just about everybody. Harry, the quiet one, doesn't usually arrive till the third or fourth race, and then it's always fun to watch the silent communication that goes on between them — raised eyebrows, pursings of lips, behind-the-hand comments, a lot of schoolboy indignance. Despite their closeness, I think they probably hate each other. They're about sixty years old and identical.

"Who've they got?"

Dale checks his clipboard. "The seven: Keepyurnose-infront."

"Forget it. I can't bet a horse with a squished name."

Dale scratches an ear. "Why do people do that? Why can't they just spell their horses' names correctly and space them normally?"

"It's because the Jockey Club won't allow horses' names to be more than eighteen letters, and that's including spaces and punctuation, so people sometimes have to crunch their horses' names to make them fit."

Dale shrugged his shoulders. "Well, what do you think, are you going to buy the twins' ticket?"

I shake my head. "I told you, I can't bet a horse with a squished name."

"I know how you feel, but you can hurt yourself that way. There've been some stellar steeds with squished names."

"I know," I say. "Itsallgreektome."

"Exactly. Songandaprayer."

"Blondeinamotel."

Dale shakes his head. "It's not like the old days when horses had classy names. Citation. War Admiral. Names that sent a shiver down your spine."

"Count Fleet," I say.

"Battle Joined."

"Whirlaway."

"Sun Beau."

"Never Bend."

"Never Say Die."

"Oh, the poetry of it," I say. I glance down at Dale's clipboard. "What else have we got in here?" I scan the entries. "Here's one. Lubbock. Now that's a not-bad name. I like just saying it. Lubbock. Big old bay gelding, probably."

"Town in Texas, if memory serves."

"Lubbock," I say, smacking my lips.

"You want to put some money on him?"

"Thank you, Dale, but I have to study the *Form* first. As soon as I've made my decision, you'll be the first to know."

SECOND RACE

POST TIME: 1:29 P.M.

(1 1/16 MILES.
3- AND 4-YEAR-OLDS.
MAIDEN SPECIAL WEIGHT.
PURSE $48,000.)

1 SPEED BUMP
2 FRISSON
3 LUBBOCK
4 DRUMMER'S KIT
5 JUDGE JOHN LEE
6 OH MY
7 KEEPYURNOSEINFRONT
8 CLEVER LAD

I step outside for a breath of air. It's cool and clear and beyond the activity of the giant yellow earth-movers and the wreckage of the old racetrack across the street, I can see the lake. Big and beautiful, and as blue as a track-odds TV screen all the way to the horizon. On the surface, at least, it's beautiful. Under the surface, so we're told, it's all zebra mussels and mercury.

An Oriental woman in a black fur coat strolls past me along the sidewalk. I often see her walking in the neighbourhood. She's usually talking on a cellphone and she's never in a hurry. I hear a screech of tires, and a black Acura speeds past. Driving like a maniac, a young Sikh boy in a white turban.

I go back inside where it's safe.

The other day I was in a bar downtown, one of those phoney English pubs that come in a kit, "The Ploughman's Arms" or "The Fox and Fiddle," something like that, one of those bars in which, despite its artificiality, I expected to feel comfortable. I was on my way to meet Anna, this woman I've been seeing lately, and I was twenty minutes early so I stopped in for a whiskey. The place was pretty much deserted except for four or five Bay Street types in three-piece suits, sitting alone at tables for two, having a drink or a late lunch — the special was steamed mussels — their attaché cases on the floor beside them. I sat at the bar and looked around at all the British clutter — the Harp and Guinness and Smithwick signs, the dartboards, the black wainscotting and red upholstery, the Freehouse and Courage and Ind Coope plaques with names like *The Ship* and *The George and Dragon* on them. But something was wrong, something seemed out of place. It could have been the skateboarding on the muted TV, but it wasn't. It was something else, something vaguely ominous. I looked around, unable to find it, and then I tuned in to the music that was playing. It was rap. Unusual in itself, American music in a "British" bar, but it was also cranked up quite loud, and I'm pretty sure the one line the lead singer — to use the term loosely — kept repeating was, "I wants to fuck you up de ass." From my vantage point at the bar I surveyed the room but no one else seemed to have noticed. One of the suits had a stunned expression on his face, but it could have been caused by any number of things: bad investments; a bad mussel.

My point being: I didn't feel safe in there.

And about ten days ago I felt unsafe in a Burger King. A short, fat, ferocious-looking server — I believe that's what they call themselves these days — became impatient when it took me a while to decide what I wanted to order; and when I finally ordered a bacon double cheeseburger, she barked, "Meal deal?" And when I said, "No, thank you, just a glass of water, please," she made a face as if she'd stepped in dog shit. Ordering a glass of water, it seems, is considered poor form. Because it's free, I suppose, or because it involves some kind of inconvenience to the staff, some kind of preparation that isn't part of their training.

"Your burger will take a few minutes," she snapped. "Stand to the side so the person behind you can order."

I said, "I'll just go find myself a table."

"I'm not bringin' it to you, if that's what you're thinkin'. Just stand to the side."

I stood there like a fool for a good five minutes until she dropped my burger and an empty cup on a tray, then looked at me as if she were expecting me to say something. Which I did. "Thank you," I said, "but the cup's empty."

Her eyes widened as if she were dealing with a imbecile, then she pointed and said, "Bever'ges is over there!"

By the time I sat down and began to eat, my hands were shaking so much I couldn't hold the two halves of the bun together in such a way as to prevent the ingredients from squeezing free, until the whole mess plopped, like a birth, onto the tray. I looked around furtively, like someone trying to dispose of an abortion. I dropped several napkins over the mess, walked quickly to the trash barrel, pulled open the door, and tilted my tray. The untouched cup of water went first, then the napkins slid off, like sheets off a corpse, but the two meat patties in their embryonic stew of mustard and catsup wouldn't budge, and, as panic prickles circled my head — the two branches straining towards each other across my forehead like a laurel — I gave the tray a violent shake, and finally the abomination hopped off and into the depths of the big black garbage bag.

Two hours later I was still shaking. Some mornings when I pull back the curtain by my bed and look outside, if the sky's overcast or if it's raining I feel so anxious there's nothing for it but to roll over and go back to sleep. If I can't sleep I'll get up and fix myself a drink.

I won't go outside all day. The thought of having to get up and wash and dress and tie my shoes and find my glasses and brush my teeth fills me with such dread that I'm pretty much paralyzed. At such times I think about Barbara, who bravely rises every morning, puts on her makeup, armors herself in her power suit, and heads off to the real estate wars. I think about how she and I used to relax, or tried to, at least — a weekend at a nice hotel downtown, room service, tickets to a musical, or we'd stay home with candlelight and wine, Keith Jarrett on the stereo. None of it worked, though, not really. I was still always tied up in knots. I couldn't relax. If I wasn't busy, I'd pace. I needed action — booze action, gambling action — and without it I'd get restless. I'd get depressed. I wouldn't return phone calls, and deadlines meant nothing to me. When people talked to me, I wouldn't answer them. Not out of rudeness; I just didn't know what to say to them. I'd stare at them like they were Martians. Barbara tried to get me to go to a shrink, but I refused. I didn't want to be told what I already knew: that I'd been steamrolled by life. So she sent me to an acupuncturist, hoping he could ease my stress. But I couldn't stand the *thought* of needles, let alone the real thing, and one treatment was all I could handle. Nothing helped. Nothing, that is, except drinking and gambling.

One of the things that kept me on the rails all those years was routine. I was a man of routine. In the mornings, for example, I always washed my face twice during my shower. My armpits and my groin I would also wash twice. Everything else once. In my closet, whichever shirt was hanging nearest to the pants was the one I was supposed to wear that morning. Because I am fortunate in that my sweat doesn't smell, I was able to wear my shirts twice before throwing them into the hamper, and in this way I could save myself from having too much laundry. After buttoning up my shirt and pulling on my pants, I would walk into the living room where I would put on my socks and shoes. I liked to do this carefully — deliberately, you might say — in a proper chair, because on more than one occasion I'd pulled a muscle or felt a vertebra slip because I hadn't been careful pulling on a sock or bending over to tie up a shoe. During the two years that I lived with Barbara, I always tried to be considerate of her — I took my shirts to the dry cleaner's rather than ask her to iron them, even though it seemed she was always ironing her own clothes — but she was not always considerate of me. In many ways she was a saint, but some mornings I would walk into the living room with a clean pair of socks in one hand and a pair of shoes in the other only to discover that the ironing board was standing in front of the wingback chair, and her exercycle was blocking the easy chair. There was nowhere to sit down except the sofa, which was too soft to sit on while putting on my socks and shoes. Sometimes Barbara even had one of her freshly ironed blouses hanging on a hanger from a handle of the sideboard, and she knew very well that's where I kept my shoehorn — right next to the Bushmills.

It's not an exaggeration to say those mornings when my routine was disrupted by Barbara's thoughtlessness did more to ruin our relationship — let alone the rest of my day — than just about anything else. They also contributed to my drinking. Sometimes I would sneak my first drink of the day right then, as I fished the shoehorn out of the sideboard, before I even had my toast and coffee. If she'd already left for the day, I might take the bottle to the kitchen table with me, where I'd be sure to find an unobstructed chair. Sometimes one drink would lead to another, and the next thing I knew it would be noon, and there I'd still be, all dressed for work but too drunk to get there.

Nowadays, in the mornings when I get up, I think about the hundreds of millions of other people in the world who wake up and stumble about trying to prepare themselves for another day of frenzied activity — the crush of the subway, bad lighting at work, no ventilation anywhere, hundreds of daily contacts with co-workers and strangers, which is very hard on people who can't even tolerate their own family — and I ask myself why bother? Why bother? And then I make myself another drink and sit down in front of the TV and turn on Maury Povich or *The View*. After I've got my fill of that, I usually get dressed and stroll over to McCully's or one of the other places I drink, or sometimes I'll go downtown without any particular plan in mind and see where I end up.

The other night for example, I staggered out of some

dive on Dundas Street — I think it was Dundas Street — and wandered over to Yonge Street to see the sights. It was unseasonably warm, and the punks, the junkies, the ginos, the skinheads, the homeless, and the whores had all come out in great numbers to enjoy it.

I stood on a corner and smoked a cigarette, then found a Swiss Chalet and snuck downstairs to use the washroom.

When I came back out to the street, two mounted policemen had guided their horses up onto the sidewalk and were talking to someone curled up in a sleeping bag. I looked at jewellery in a store window and thought briefly about Barbara. When I started up the street again, the mounted policemen were ahead of me. A low-slung Nissan was stopped at the curb, and the driver, a young man with his baseball cap turned sideways, had his flashers on and the volume up so high on his radio that the concrete under my feet seemed to pulse with the beat. When one of the policemen maneuvered his horse to within inches of the driver's window, leaned down in his saddle and banged on the glass with his nightstick, the young man practically jumped out of his seat, quickly turned down the volume, and lowered his window. The policeman said, "You're in a 'No Stopping' zone, move your car." "I'm waiting for my friend," the young man said. "He's in there." He jerked his thumb in the direction of a pizza parlour. The policeman nudged his horse so that it blocked the front of the car. His partner moved his horse to the back. The first policeman removed his summons book from his belt, flipped it open, glanced down at the Nissan's license plate, and began to write. "Hey, what are you doing?" the young man protested, his head halfway out the window. The policeman said, "Which part of 'Move your car' didn't you understand?"

When I heard that, I laughed out loud. Beside me an east Indian man pushing a dark-eyed little girl in a stroller had also stopped to watch. My laughter attracted the attention of the second policeman's horse, and it swung its enormous head around until it was only inches from the little girl's face, with the result that she screamed so shrilly the policeman lurched in his saddle, the horse blinked and rotated its ears, and I, in my haste to get away from the appalling noise, nearly flattened a tiny Chinese man who was standing on the other side of me.

A few blocks north, waiting for the lights to change at College Street, I found myself eavesdropping on a middle-aged African-American couple. It wasn't their accent that gave them away, it was their appearance. They were wearing bright expensive clothes, matching windbreakers, lots of jewellery, and the woman's hair was dark red and swept around her head in a garish style I associate with black American women. They were discussing which way they should walk to get back to their hotel, and when I asked if they were lost, the woman said, "As a matter of fact, we are. We're a pair of lost exhausted tourists!" I asked which hotel they were staying at, then explained how to get there. They thanked me and were just about to resume their journey when I mentioned how much I love the States, and especially American corner bars, and asked them if they would like to visit a typical neighbourhood bar right here in Toronto. The man demurred, but the woman said, "Oh, Ray, don't be such a poop, it's our last night!" I hailed a cab, and when we were seated in the back, the woman, who was between her husband and me, said, "It feels so good to rest my dogs."

Fifteen minutes later I was sitting on my corner stool at McCully's with the American couple on the two stools to my right. Anticipating a free drink — the Americans paid for the cab — I asked Dexter for a double Bushmills and a pint of Creemore. The man asked for a Budweiser, and the woman a Diet Pepsi. At first, the conversation was cordial — they complimented me on my city, how safe it was compared to Detroit — but then I became aware of the sound of my own voice and the silence of the woman, who had been quite chatty earlier, and the concentration her husband was giving the label of his beer bottle. I quit whatever I was saying, excused myself, spent several minutes calming down in the washroom, and when I returned to the bar the man and woman were gone.

"Where'd they go?" I asked Dexter.

Dexter shrugged his shoulders. "All I know is they paid for their drinks and left."

"Was I rude to them?"

"You did say a couple of things that might have made them uncomfortable feel a bit uncomfortable."

"What'd I say?"

"Well, for starters, you told them George Bush was a moron."

"He *is* a moron," I said, reaching for the man's half-finished beer.

"Yes, but then you went on to say that anybody who voted for someone with eyes that close together had to be a moron, too."

"Oh. Did they pay for my drinks?"

Dexter gave me his disapproving look. "Yes, they paid for your drinks."

Back inside, I resume my seat at the bar and take a long pull on my pint.

I make my deliberations. I decide on Judge John Lee because even though he's never won a race in his life, he's been in the money five of his twelve starts, he was beat a neck and a head at the same track, same distance, same class, when he tried to steal it on the engine in August, and he's got a promising bugboy by the name of Nguyen in the irons, so he's in light at 105 pounds. Also, he's 3-1 on the board, which sweetens the mix even more. The twins' horse is 4-5. I get off my stool and make my way over to Dale.

"Dale, ten across on the five-horse, please."

I hand him thirty dollars and he says, "Ten across on numero cinco. Duly noted."

"Did the twins sell their ticket?"

Dale smiles. "No, it's only a two-dollar ticket, and they're asking twenty."

"Twenty! The morning line had Keepyurschnozzinfront at two to one, which as you and I know means he's going to end up odds-on. Should he actually win, they'll be lucky if the Double *pays* twenty."

"Tell *them* that."

On my way back to the bar I pass the twins. They're standing at the island, each with a half-gone pint of lite in front of him. I think they even drink at the same pace. "Harry," I say. "Ronny. Rumour has it you've got a Double ticket for sale."

They give each other a crafty look. Then Ronny says, "We've got the seven."

"Keepyurdickinfront?"

"Keepyur*nose*infront, actually," says Ronny.

"How much you want for it?" I ask.

"Twenty dollars."

"Too much."

They confer. Ronny says, "How much will you offer?"

I stroke my chin. "Two dollars."

Identical insulted looks appear on their faces. "That's ridiculous," says Harry, speaking for the first time. "That's what we paid for the ticket."

"Lighten up, fellas," I say. "But seriously, even if your horse does win, the Double won't pay more than thirty for two. Thirty-five tops."

"Take it or leave it," says Ronny.

I shake my head. "Where did you boys grow up?"

Back on my stool I ask Dexter for a shot of Bushmills. The very first time I asked him for a shot of Bushmills, he told me he didn't carry it. There wasn't much call for it, he said. So I made him a proposition. If I buy the Bushmills, I told him, and you keep it under the bar for me, I'll pay you corkage every time you pour me a shot. So he said okay, and it's worked out well. Corkage comes to whatever I feel like tipping him, basically. Fifty cents, usually. He always lets me know when I need to replenish — "You're running low on that Bullshit, Mr. Harvey" — and I go out and buy another couple of bottles. It's a little expensive this way, but at least I know where I can get a shot of good Irish whiskey when I need it.

Judge John Lee breaks on top. The bugboy shakes the reins a couple of times, and before the announcer has even begun his call they're out front by two. They motor along for an eighth of a mile, then the boy takes him under wraps, standing in the irons, the whip tucked under his armpit. He slows the pace: twenty-four; forty-nine and three. Nobody wants to press the issue, which is exactly what I'd hoped. The other horses gallop along as a group behind him, waiting for him to tire. Into the far turn he's out front by six, and he's still got plenty. By the head of the stretch it looks like it's over. Judge John Lee in front by five. But then the six horse, Oh My, starts to move. The boy steals a glance under his arm, and seeing it's going to be a horse race after all, takes out his whip and whacks Judge John Lee eight or ten times on the hindquarters. Judge John Lee picks it up a bit, and the other horse, sensing he's beat even though he's closed two more lengths, starts to quit, but Judge John Lee's ears prick back and he starts to flatten out, no more drive left in him. The other jockey waves his whip in front of Oh My's right eye, and they're back in business, and he's coming on strong, the bugboy whaling away at Judge John Lee's flank, nothing left in the tank, the other horse at his bootstraps, his shoulder, his neck, but happily, happily, that's when they hit the wire. Two jumps later and Oh My's in front, but it's too late, all's well, the good guys win again. Judge John Lee by a head. I watch closely as the rest of the field crosses the finish line, and I see what I want to see, the only thing that could make this victory sweeter: Keepyurnoseinfrontfinisheslast.

The numbers go up: $8.60, $6.30, $4.30. Very nice. Times five all of them and, let's see, I collect ninety-six smackers. Less $30 for the bet. And a deuce for Dale. I net $64. Plus the $47 from the first race means I'm up $111. Well, truth be told, I'm up $61, less Anna's fifty which is safe in my pocket.

File Oh My for next time.

The Double I didn't bet but would have won if I'd remembered in time pays $59 and change.

On my way over to collect, I pass the twins again. They're both smoking Benson and Hedges. Pip pip. Because I wouldn't buy their losing Double ticket, they lift their noses and look away as I pass them. Their little red rabbit eyes. My guess is they live together. My guess is they have matching pajamas and spank each other at bedtime.

Thinking about the twins just now reminded me of another unsafe situation I found myself in when I was just starting out as a racetrack journalist and *Sport of Kings* sent me down to Finger Lakes Race Track, and one day when there was no racing I got in my car and five hours later ended up in a bar called the Jolly Roger in Lake George, and a serious-looking man in his early forties sat down beside me and started a conversation.

As I recall, we talked about music mostly, and Vietnam — this was the early seventies, after all. He was broad-shouldered, six foot, one-eighty or thereabouts, with a thick, black beard. When he found out I had a two-hundred-and-fifty-mile drive back to Canandaigua, he invited me to crash at his place in Glen's Falls, half an hour away. I got in my car and followed him.

In his apartment he gave me a beer and showed me a photograph of his nephew and told me the boy had been run over by a dump truck a year earlier. I remember I was still studying the photograph when his telephone rang, and he went into the next room to take it. I could still hear his voice through the closed door, and that's when I realized he was gay. He must have been talking to another gay, because his voice was different than when he'd been talking to me.

When he came back into the living room, I had my ass to the wall. I probably had a deer-in-the-headlights look on my face, too, but he didn't try anything. To tell the truth, I don't really think he was after sex at all. Well, maybe if he'd thought I was into it, but he must have come to the conclusion that I was just a dumb kid who needed a place to sleep, and that was the end of it. He was just being decent.

I slept on the sofa. In the morning he was gone. There was a box of cereal on the kitchen table, and a bowl and spoon, and there may have been a note wishing me a safe journey, but I can't be sure about that part of it. There was definitely a parking ticket under the wiper of my car when I got outside. I still have it — somewhere in the top drawer of my dresser where I keep the postcards, photographs, matchbooks, ticket stubs, newspaper clippings, and all the other detritus of my life.

One of my many shortcomings is that I watch a lot of daytime TV. I shouldn't, I know I shouldn't, because it just confirms my cynical view of the world. Like a fat man sitting down to a tray of Twinkies, I hate myself for doing it, but in a weird way it's the right thing to do. It's one of those defining activities. Every once in a while you have to identify yourself, you have to remind yourself who you are, either by inhaling a dozen Twinkies, or, in my case, by watching tabloid TV, which will once again confirm my low opinion of mankind. The sad parade: people so fat from all the Twinkies they've eaten in their lives that they get stuck in doorways; pregnant teenagers, white supremacist teenagers, teenagers into body piercing, tattooing, and intentional scarring. Their trashy lives made legitimate by an appearance on *Jerry Springer*. And the studio audience shamelessly offering their opinions and their advice and their judgments. Thank God, they think to themselves — if they're capable of thinking — at last I've found someone worse off than me. Their eyes pop, their jaws drop as the stage fills with New Age freaks. What I want to know is whatever happened to Lobster Boy and The Bearded Lady?

Whatever happened to The Man with Elastic Skin?

Watching bad TV is only one of the many flaws in my makeup. My good qualities, on the other hand, are few. An example: because my sweat doesn't smell I can wear the same shirt for days, and there will be no body odour whatsoever. During the hottest stretch of last summer while, coincidentally, I was on an extended losing streak, I wore the same navy blue T-shirt two weeks running. I even slept in it. Finally someone — probably Anna — said, "What are those marks on your shirt?" I looked down. I had these twin, white, salt-encrusted sweat stains over my kidneys. But you know what? The shirt didn't smell. I've washed that shirt a dozen times since, and you can still see the perimeters of those sweat stains. They look like the islands of Western Samoa.

When racehorses get kidney sweat, however, it is — in my opinion — a bad sign. When people ask my advice on the subject, I tell them to watch the post parade, and if the horse they like's got kidney sweat — a white lather between his back legs — lay off him. It means he's nervous or upset. Of course, some people argue the other way; the horse will fairly fly when the gate springs. A trainer by the name of Snelling, at one of the B-Tracks I covered many years ago, would take a two-foot length of garden hose to his horses' muzzles just before they were led to the saddling enclosure. He wanted them ready to run. They were so scared they had plenty of kidney sweat. And sometimes they won. I remember a dead gelding in one of Snelling's stalls one time. It must have died of a heart attack after being beaten, but I never said anything, and so far as I know nobody else did, either.

The day I got fired, I was at home trying to remember the title of a tune I'd been wanting to listen to, when the phone rang. Reed, my boss at *Sport of Kings*, said, "Why aren't you here?"

"I'm looking for something," I said.

"It's eleven o'clock in the fucking morning," Reed said. "This is the fourth time this month you haven't shown up, and you know what?"

"What?" I said.

"It's only the tenth. It's only the tenth of November, and already you've failed to show up for work four times. That's eight work days, and you've failed to show up for *half* of them!"

"Sorry," I said.

"And on those rare occasions when you *do* show up, you're always late. What gives?"

Then I remembered the title. "Reed, do you own a CD player?"

"Do I own a what?"

"A CD player. A compact disc player. They more or less replaced record players about ten years ago."

"Why are you talking about CD players?"

"Those of us who *do* own CD players have a sacred and rather expensive obligation to replace all our old favourite LPs with CDs."

"Does this have anything to do with you not being at work today?"

"I'm searching for a particular CD," I said. "*Mingus at Carnegie Hall*." I could picture the cover: a triptych of black and white photos of Charles Mingus in a dark suit and wide-brimmed black hat bent over his bass. "I've lost it. I've searched high and low."

"Who the fuck's Mingus?"

"Just the most important bassist in the history of jazz music, that's who."

"How much have you had to drink?"

"In my life?" I began to laugh.

The upshot of the conversation was that I lost my job. After thirty-one years of writing articles for *Sport of Kings*, the bastards fired me. They'd fired me before — three or four times — but this time it stuck. It wasn't just Reed, I know that. He didn't have the authority. No, it came down from Head Office in Chicago. "Run that drunk's ass," some suit said.

I dropped the phone and wandered around a while longer looking for Charles Mingus. I'd bought the CD, a reissue of a 1974 LP, a few weeks earlier. There were only two cuts on it: "Perdido" (21:57) and "C Jam Blues" (24:37). I knew that concert like the back of my hand. I knew when the trumpeter, Jon Faddis, tipped his musical hat to Dizzy Gillespie. I knew when tenor great Roland Kirk parodied the young sax player George Adams, "cuttin' him at his own shit," to quote the liner notes. "C Jam Blues" was the tune I wanted to hear.

At one point in my search I found myself staring at my reflection in the long mirror on the inside of the hall closet door. The pink terrycloth robe I was wearing (I believe it once belonged to a woman named Lois) was unbelted and hung open, revealing a pair of pale green boxer shorts. Except for brown socks, I was otherwise naked. When I peered closely at my face, I was shocked: my hair was shaggy and uncombed and greyer than I remembered it, with streaks of old-man yellow in it that made me look like I was rotting from the inside out; the skin of my face was like parchment;

my eyes were rheumy and red-veined. There was something in them that made me nervous; the word "dissipation" springs to mind. I panned down the too-short sleeves of the dressing gown, past my thin wrists, to my hands. One held an unlit cigarette, the other a half-gone mickey of Silk Tassel in the shatter-proof plastic bottle recommended by alcoholics everywhere. Normally I don't drink the cheap stuff, but maybe I'd had a premonition that I was soon to be unemployed and had already begun to budget.

"Dexter."

"Yes, Mr. Harvey?"

"A Creemore, please. And send a Budweiser over to Dale. I've touched him twice and it's not even the third yet."

A wash of light sweeps through the bar, and we all turn our heads to see who's coming in. It's two uniformed police officers from 56. I swivel on my stool to look for Dale, but he's already retired from the field. At the same time as I fold my *Form* and slip it inside my jacket, Dexter aims the remote at TV #1 and the blue track-odds screen is replaced by the image of a Mediterranean-looking man standing in a kitchen silently addressing the camera. He's wearing an apron and a chef's hat and holds a spatula in one hand.

One of the uniforms sidles over to where I'm sitting. "Good to see you again, Mr. Harvey. How you doing?"

"Badge number, please."

The uniform makes a sour face and says, "Three three six five nine."

"Thank you. To what do we owe the pleasure of your company?"

"Routine patrol, is all. Why, anything you want to tell us about?"

"Like what?"

"Any excitement of any kind?"

I consider his question. "Dexter had to eighty-six a guy."

"That's nice, but I —"

"Scar on his cheek like a bullet hole."

"— I was thinking more along the lines of have you noticed anything like illegal commerce in here this afternoon?"

I shake my head. "Can't say that I have. The only commerce I've witnessed has been entirely legal. I give Dexter money, he gives me alcohol."

"Nothing in the way of bookmaking going on?"

I cast my gaze around the room and shake my head again. "See for yourself."

He looks up at TV #1. "Didn't realize the crowd in here was such big fans of *Emeril*. Lots of interest in gourmet cooking, is there?"

He moves off down the bar, talks to another of the regulars, then he and his partner leave a minute or two later.

I swivel so I'm facing front again. Cops make me nervous, and my hands are shaking. I concentrate on how Dexter has all the liquor bottles lined up and facing front on their shelves behind the bar. They look like proud little soldiers, their chests out, their labels displayed. I'm just starting to calm down when Jessy appears at my ear. She of the green eyes and red hair. A bit of a belly, but hey. "Dale says thanks for the beer," she whispers, "and wants you to note the eight horse in the next race."

I scan down the entries for the third race in my *Form*. Number eight is Red Scout. I turn on my stool and peer through the crowd. I have to wait till several people pass by in front of me before I can see that Dale is back at his station, smiling at me. I smile back. The steed he mentioned, ancient now by racehorse standards at eleven years of age, was a particular favourite of a man he and I had a lot of time for: a hard-drinking Irishman named Finn Boyle.

THIRD RACE

Post Time: 1:58 p.m.

(6 Furlongs.
4-Year-Olds and Up.
Claiming $25,000.
Purse $32,000.)

1 Tapas
2 Havalook
3 Rhodes II
4 Motoring
5 Good Things Come
6 Steep Climb
7 Orion's Belt
8 Red Scout

The stool at the corner of the bar is prime. This is true at most bars, but none more so than McCully's. If you're sitting on the corner stool at McCully's and you look past the two stools to your left and the Infinity video poker game next to them, you have a clear view of the main door to the street, and you can see who's coming in and who's going out. If you swivel a hundred and eighty degrees on your stool, you can watch through the large front windows the snail-slow dismantling of the old racetrack across the road. Another quarter turn, and you're looking at the big-screen TV on the far wall and the ATM machine and pay phone next to the doorway that leads into the lobby of the Hearth&Home Hotel. If you resume your normal position at the bar and look slightly to your right, you'll see the island where the twins always stand, then the booths, and, beyond them, the pool table and the dance floor with its little karaoke stage. And if you look straight ahead down the length of the bar, through the tunnel created by the faces of the drinkers on your right and the ornamental draft handles opposite them — the lion's head, the hockey stick, the ace of spades — you'll see Jessy at the cash register, and, above her head, the dangling Lucky Draw Muskoka chair, and, just past her, the patio umbrella that an enterprising beer salesman convinced Vinnie, the manager, to set up inside the bar, complete with white plastic table and chairs.

I didn't properly move into McCully's until a year ago, when Barbara left and I established myself on the corner stool. In the old days — and now I'm going back fifteen, twenty years — the corner stool was occupied, kinglike, by a series of Runyonesque horse-players and other shady characters with names like Al the Hat, Stand Alone, Big Clare, and Finn Boyle, so I was honoured when it was suggested to me — by Finn Boyle, no less — that I assume it. What made the gesture especially meaningful was that at the time Finn Boyle was said stool's occupant, but he was going away for a while and didn't want it tenanted by just anyone.

When I first made his acquaintance, Finn Boyle lived upstairs in the Hearth&Home. This is not the sort of antiseptic, impersonal Hearth&Home you're used to seeing near the airports of most North American cities. No, this one is a fleabag and a fire trap. It was purchased three years ago from the D'Attilio family. Vinnie's a D'Attilio. For some reason he stayed on after the rest of the family moved to Pompano Beach. As I said earlier, it was the Grove Hotel when they owned it, and it was even seedier then. It featured striptease, drug deals, and biker fights. The reason Hearth&Home bought it was because of the racetrack across the street. The now abandoned and lifeless racetrack across the street. Where once you would smell the fragrance of horse manure wafting through the open door of McCully's Tavern on a Saturday afternoon, now you smell sewage and car exhaust. Where once you could hear the bell of the starting gate and the distant thunder of hooves, now you hear the honking of car alarms and the voices of passersby as they shout into their cellphones. And where once you could sit high and alone in the grandstand at Dundas Park and watch the morning workouts — the horses materializing out of the mist at the head of the stretch, the clockers hunched like owls at the rail — now all you can do is peer through a hole in the plywood barricade they've erected along the sidewalk and watch the faded green paint flaking off the tote board and ugly weeds rearing up like triffids through the soil of the track itself. It's been like this for two years now — a slow destruction. Somebody at Hearth&Home didn't do his or her homework: he or she recommended that Hearth&Home purchase the Grove Hotel, the deal was done, the racetrack closed down a year later, the anticipated hordes of American gamblers in town for the spring and fall thoroughbred meets never materialized, the D'Attilios turned nut-brown in the Florida sun, and the few guests of the hotel nowadays are mostly the same transients who lived here when it was the Grove, and who live here the first couple of weeks of each month until their welfare dries up, but who are happier transients than they used to be because the bikers and druggies are gone and there's fresh paint on the walls of their rooms and new carpets on the floors. Once in a while a brightly dressed family of tourists from Ohio or Quebec washes up here at the end of a long day of theme-parking, but even though the tableau they present as they stand at the front desk — exhausted, burdened with bags, expressions of controlled horror on their faces — amuses us, we don't bother them, and they're always gone by the time the regular residents shuffle through the lobby late the next morning, scratching themselves on their way to the bar.

When I knew him, Finn Boyle was making his living as a professional victim. About a year before he washed up on this particular beach, he had a job in a factory and was about a decade away from a comfortable pension. One day there was an accident — a piece of machinery went flying — and Finn Boyle was blinded in his right eye. He was put on temporary disability until it was determined that the blindness was permanent. Then he was put on permanent disability. Then he sued his employer for unsafe working conditions. Then his wife left him because she couldn't stand him moping around the house all day.

A few months later he was walking along Queen Street with a patch over his eye and didn't see a woman with a minivan full of kids making a left turn into the Burger King at the corner of Horton Avenue. The minivan hit him, and Finn Boyle was thrown fifty feet into the drive-thru menu. His left hip was broken and also his left leg, in three places. He was in hospital for eight weeks. Then he got the lawyer he had hired to handle the lawsuit against his former employers to file a lawsuit against the driver of the car, her insurance company, and Burger King. Then the doctors at the hospital decided to try a cornea transplant to correct Finn Boyle's eyesight, but it got botched somehow and Finn Boyle's blind eye was not only still blind, but it bulged like a frog's. So he sued the hospital, too.

For the year or so that I knew him, Finn Boyle was a cantankerous son of a bitch. The Greek fisherman's hat and goatee he sported and the prized black oak walking stick he never let out of his sight couldn't make up for that reptilian right eye which he refused to cover with a patch because, he told me, he wanted the world to see what had been done to him. As for the walking stick, local legend has it that Finn Boyle was limping along Queen Street one afternoon shortly after his release from hospital, when a limousine slowed down beside him, one of the tinted rear windows lowered, and a beautiful young woman — a fashion model, by some accounts — handed him the walking stick. When I first heard the story, I asked myself what a beautiful young woman would be doing with a walking stick, and so when I finally got to know Finn Boyle well enough, I asked him if there was any truth to the tale. It was true, he claimed, except that the woman in the limousine was far from young and beautiful; on the contrary, she was old, veined, and bejewelled.

While he was waiting for the results of his lawsuits, Finn Boyle lived at the Hearth&Home. And while he was waiting, he was betting a lot of money he couldn't afford to lose, but was losing anyway. This made him even more cantankerous. According to Dexter, Finn Boyle usually came down from his room about ten-thirty in the morning and seated himself at the corner of the bar; he'd be there at noon when I arrived, and he'd still be there at midnight when I headed home. Finn Boyle loved exactors, couldn't stay away from them, but he was always just missing, finishing first/third, or second/third. I suggested to him one time that he lay off the exotics and just bet straight — win, place, show. He turned red, his mouth went into a kind of rictus, that ugly eye looked about ready to pop, and he said, "How I bet is nobody's business but my own, so how 'bout you just fuck off!" For a moment I was afraid he was going to wrap that walking stick around my neck.

And it was just about then, when Finn Boyle's fortunes were at their lowest — lawsuits in limbo and a spell of bad gambling — that the cops busted the bookies at McCully's.

It was last May, about six weeks into the spring meet, and business was so brisk that the bookies catered a Kentucky Derby buffet right here in McCully's. Anna was with me that day, and when we walked into the bar it was a surprise to see all this food set out on platters — cold cuts and chicken wings, carrots and celery and sweet pickles, rye bread and fresh buns from Silverstein's — and people wearing party hats and blowing into those things that squawk and unfurl. Dale came up to me and said, "Mr. Harvey, welcome to the feast." He looked at Anna, whom he had never seen before, and dipped his head. "And your beautiful lady is welcome, too. This is me and Consensus and Ringo's way of saying thank you." It was a memorable afternoon, full of good cheer and camaraderie, and it was topped off by the Run for the Roses itself, won by a Cinderella colt called Smarty Jones.

But word must have gotten around about the big party at McCully's because the next day — Sunday — when I arrived about noon, two strangers were sitting at the far end of the bar, near the promotional umbrella, and right away I marked them. For one thing, they were drinking coffee, a dead giveaway at McCully's. Everyone else marked them as well, so Dale was just sitting there reading, and the gamblers — Finn Boyle among them — were making small talk about politics and the hockey playoffs. And everything was cool. Except the cops were in no hurry to leave. The races were legally televised on Sundays, and we all watched the first race on TV #1 as if we could care less. But those among us who had picked the winner started to simmer. Finn Boyle in particular.

Half an hour later, the second race went, and the cops were still sitting there, nursing their coffees. People were getting agitated. The guys who had picked the Double were noticeably unhappy by this point. Tics were acting up. People were pulling at their hair and muttering under their breath and ordering a steady stream of bar shots. Some were pacing around pulling their fingers, or going outside only to come right back in.

Finn Boyle hadn't moved from his stool. At first, he'd participated in the small talk, but by now — two races in — his face was a deep glowing maroon and his froggy eye was pulsating as if it were radioactive.

Then the third race went, and when a horse called Precocious won by eight lengths at 8-1 and a 57-1 shot finished second, setting up a six-hundred-dollar exactor, Finn Boyle climbed carefully down from his stool at the end of the bar and made his slow, hobbling way through the crowd towards the cops, who were just now doctoring their umpteenth cups of coffee. With the knobbed end of his walking stick, he tapped one of the cops on the shoulder and then wearily, like a man who knows he's about to do something that's going to cost him big time, but he just has to do it anyway because it's the principle of the thing, said, "I had it on good authority that Precocious was going to win that race. I was going to key him with all the other horses in the race. I would definitely have had that exactor. Plus, I had the winner of the first and the winner of the second and the Double, and very likely I would have nailed the exactors in both races. This would have been my comeback day. But you and your partner ruined that. Him and you have cost me probably six grand. Eight, maybe. So I have an idea. How about you and him get the fuck out of here before I go crazy on you. Did you really think we didn't know who you were? Are you that stupid? With your shiny new sneakers and your schoolboy haircuts? You look like you belong to Heaven's Gate, for fucksake. Put that coffee down — you too, Columbo — and get the fuck out of here before I take this cane and ram it up *both* your asses!"

They arrested him. They dragged him kicking and screaming out to their car and threw him in the back and took him downtown. Later, I saw his walking stick on the floor near the karaoke stage, and I picked it up and gave it to Dexter for safekeeping. When I think back on it now, I wish we'd all climbed down off our stools and stopped the cops from roughing Finn Boyle up like that. After all, a broken hip, a leg broken in three places, a blind eye protruding like a golf ball, no wife, no job, no home, and a bad betting streak. But we just sat there on our hands and watched this guy, who had ten times the balls of any of us, get treated like that. But hey, that's why most of us are here — because we've stopped fighting. We'd sooner just look away. We'd sooner just order another drink. On the surface, the community I live in is friendly enough, but as soon as trouble arrives it's every man for himself. We all know that. Finn Boyle knew it, too.

The next day, Monday, the same two cops came back, only this time they had two more with them. They marched straight through the bar and into the kitchen, and there was a lot of yelling and pot-banging, and when they came out they marched straight back through the bar and out the door.

Then Vinnie came out of the kitchen and told Dale he had to leave and not to come back, and to pass the message along to Consensus and Ringo. Vinnie hated to do it, of course — not least of all because the bookies brought in lots of hard-drinking customers and paid him a stipend, too — but the cops had left him no choice.

So they left, and everyone was kind of sad, and we all moved down the street to the Diamond, which we don't like as much, but which we had to make do with until the dust settled. Because it's a much smaller operation, the Diamond can only support one bookie, and because Dale is the elder statesman of the three, the other two were basically out of work, and I kept bumping into one or the other walking aimlessly along Queen Street looking frazzled and homeless. They kept trying to sell me stuff — shampoo, a nine iron, a case of hot sauce. For a while, Consensus sold clothes — sweat suits and jeans, mostly. People would give him their sizes and tell him what they wanted, then he would somehow acquire the clothes — probably off the back of a truck — and bring them to the Diamond where the people who'd ordered them would pick them up and pay him. Ringo approached me on the sidewalk one afternoon, pushing a lawnmower. He reached down and pulled the cord and it started. I had to shout over the noise, "Ringo, I don't even own a house, let alone a lawn."

* * *

No, Finn Boyle had more balls than any of us and he wasn't shy about telling you what he thought of you.

One night, a couple of months before the bookies got busted, we were sitting here betting the jugheads at Mohawk — Finn Boyle on the stool at the end of the bar, me next to him — when we became aware of a lot of noise emanating from the booths. At one point the noise was so loud that Dexter had to turn up the volume on TV #1 so we could hear the call of a race. Finn Boyle lost some money on the race and his mood went decidedly grim. Then this raucous laughter erupted out of the booths again, and Finn Boyle asked who was making all the noise. Dexter said it was a slo-pitch team. Finn Boyle turned to me. "You're pretty knowledgeable, right? Isn't slo-pitch sort of like T-ball, only it's for adults? Isn't slo-pitch basically a game for assholes? Come on with me, let's meet some of these slo-pitch assholes." Finn Boyle got off his stool, grabbed his walking stick, and followed the laughter through the crowded, smoky bar to its source.

Eight or ten ballplayers in maroon-and-white uniforms were squeezed into two booths. And — surprise, surprise — they were all women! And these were no ballerinas, these were big, strong girls. As they turned to look at Finn Boyle, who was banging his walking stick on the floor for attention, I read TOMCO WELDING AND FABRICATING across their chests. The numbers on the backs of the sweaters of the women facing away from us were ridiculously small: a tiny white 8 on a vast maroon field, a tiny 3, a tiny 2.

"Ladies, ladies," Finn Boyle said when they were all looking at him, "what with all the racket you're making, we can't hear ourselves *think* over at the bar, let alone talk, so how about you just shut the fuck up?"

The woman closest to us stood up. If her teammates were big, she was huge. Once she was standing she hitched up her trousers, cowboy-style. She had a good sixty pounds on Finn Boyle, and sported a crewcut mullet. "I think maybe you got things upside down, buster," she said, and poked him in the chest.

"Now, hold everything," Finn Boyle said, taking an involuntary step backwards, "I'm a man with a cane."

"I think maybe *you're* the one needs to shut the fuck up," she said, forcing Finn Boyle farther back. "I think maybe *you* should find yourself someplace to crawl inside of and die."

When Finn Boyle was backed right up against the island, he said, "Don't get me wrong, lady, I got nothing against your type. We just want a little quiet here so's we can watch the races."

The woman put her hands on her hips, her gigantic bosom rising like bread. "You've got nothing against our *type*?"

By now everyone in McCully's was watching. The gamblers, the dart players, the pool players. Dexter and Jessy. The twins — huddled under the promotional umbrella like a couple of golfers caught in a rainstorm.

Finn Boyle cleared his throat. "What I mean is, I'm not, like, offended by your sexual orientation, I just —"

"You got any children, jerk-off?"

This stopped Finn Boyle cold. He considered the question, then said, "They live with their mother."

"You got a daughter?"

"Yeah, a boy and a girl, but I don't see what my having children has to do with —"

"How would you like it if your daughter was a dyke?" the woman said, thrusting her face into Finn Boyle's. "What would you do then?"

Finn Boyle's complexion went from pink to scarlet. "You're skating on thin ice, lady, or whatever you are. You'd better clear out of here before I go crazy on you."

The woman's face went scarlet, too. "With a father like you, it's very likely she *will* go dyke. In fact, she's probably *already* dyke! And if your son ain't already a flamer, it's only a matter of time!"

The women in the booths screamed with laughter. "Fuckin' A, Rosey!" someone yelled, and "Go, girl!" But they quit when Finn Boyle seized a pint of beer off the island and flung it in the woman's face. Then, faster than I'd ever seen him move, Finn Boyle was smashing the knob of his walking stick down on beer glasses and baseball mitts and baskets of chicken wings. He picked up a full pitcher of beer and hurled the contents across the faces of five of the women. You've never seen two packed booths empty so fast in your life. Then, just as they were about to tear Finn Boyle to pieces, Dexter waded into the melee, put Finn Boyle in a headlock, steered him through a gauntlet of drinkers and through the door to the Hearth&Home lobby. I was hard on their heels when Dexter yelled, "Lock it!" As I turned and bolted the door behind me, several of the women's faces squished together in the small rectangular window.

"Let me go!" Finn Boyle yelled, struggling to get free, still swinging his walking stick. "I'll kill the whore. I'll rip her damn arms off!"

"Goddamn it, Finn," Dexter said fiercely, "it's bad enough you attack a patron, but did you have to pick

Vinnie's cousin?"

Finn Boyle stopped struggling. He twisted his neck and looked up at Dexter from the headlock. "Vinnie's cousin?"

"That's right," Dexter said. He released Finn Boyle and said, "Rosey D'Attilio. I could lose my job over this. Now get up to your room before they break down the door. And don't let me see your face for a week."

One time, I had the privilege of being thrown out of a bar *with* Finn Boyle.

We were half in the bag at a strip club called Gents. They had table dancers there, and Finn Boyle kept trying to hire one, but he said such rude things to them that they would pick up their little stools and totter away on their high heels before we got to see anything. I tried to hush him, but he just growled and barked at me. So, when no more girls would come to our table, Finn Boyle stood up and started dancing and undressing himself and had managed to remove his down vest and had peeled off his sleeveless black muscle shirt before a couple of bouncers seized him by the arms and dragged him off towards the door. I picked up his shirt and vest and hurried after them, pleading Finn Boyle's case. "Only having a little fun, boys," I said. Finn Boyle said, "All I was doing was disrobing, that's what people do in here is disrobe, it's not like I had my pecker in my hand, you fuckers!" One of the bouncers said to me, "You're gone, too, buddy," and before we knew it we were outside, the door slammed shut behind us, and it was winter and cold as hell. I handed Finn Boyle his clothes, and as he pulled the muscle shirt over his head, he said, "Come on, I've got a plan," and led me across the street and behind a billboard. "Now give me your hat, Mr. Harvey, and your glasses, and

I'll give you my scarf and cane. And give me your coat." He passed me his down vest, which smelled vaguely of urine, and I gingerly slid my arms through the arm-holes. He put on the jacket of my white plantation suit and tugged my Panama hat down to his eyebrows. He tucked the arms of my bifocals behind his ears and marched in circles with his hands in front of him like a blind man. I put on his fluorescent pink, foam-padded trucker's hat that said DO IT IN A TENT across the front and wound his tartan scarf around my neck. He handed me his walking stick and said, "They'll never recognize us. Let's go."

We marched straight back across the street and into Gents.

As soon as they saw us, the bouncers closed in. They weren't fooled for a second. Finn Boyle called for his walking stick. I tossed it to him, and he dropped it. Then they were all over us, Finn Boyle shouting, "Where's me shillelagh?" They gave us the bum's rush to the door and propelled us across the sidewalk with such force that we slid on our faces through the slush. I sat up in the gutter and watched Finn Boyle's pink hat sailing towards us from the doorway. Then his walking stick clattered down beside me, the door slammed shut for the second time, and we were left there in the cold and wet and dark.

We stood up, brushed ourselves off and started walking. I don't remember much after that except Finn Boyle making a call from a phone booth on Euphala Avenue, followed shortly thereafter by advancing sirens, a fleet of fire and rescue trucks headed in the direction of Gents, us running like schoolboys down an alleyway full of cats and garbage cans, and my discovery the next morning of a bruise on the inside of my left biceps the size and colour of a plum.

* * *

I stayed away from Gents for a while after that, but sometimes a man gets lonely, and if there's no woman in his life, or if there is but she's unavailable, or out of sorts, or unkindly disposed towards him, and if he knows that his need is a little more extreme than the latest issue of *Hustler* or his favourite video can satisfy, then the man might just throw caution to the wind and go where he probably shouldn't.

So, a few weeks after Finn Boyle and I were thrown out of Gents, I went back one night by myself. For twenty minutes or so I watched the featured dancers on stage. One of them was dressed in leopard skin, another in lingerie, and the third in a cheerleader's outfit, complete with pom-poms.

The first lap dancer I hired at my table was dressed like a private school girl. She shouted in my ear that her name was Valerie. While she was gyrating above me — I was sitting in a chair, my hands gripping its arms — I asked her where she was from. California, she said, via New York. She was tall and blonde and probably a liar and had large, enhanced breasts. She went on to tell me about the break-up of her parents' marriage, and the fight over who got the Mercedes, and how her father was so much older than her mother, and how a year later her mother took up with a man fifteen years younger than she was, and how her mother was presently with a man exactly her own age, and how maybe this time she'd got it right. Then she altered her position so I had a good view of her pussy. Even though there wasn't much light where I was sitting, I could make out the row of gold rings in her labia. I asked about them, and she referred to them as her "chastity belt," which made me wonder whether she had to remove them in order to have sex. There must have been a dozen of them. Anyway, she kept thrusting her pussy into my face, until I said, "Go easy with that, will you," which must have offended her because as soon as the song ended she got dressed and left without so much as a fare-thee-well.

Valerie had cost me twenty dollars. I moved back to the bar and ordered a beer and a shot of rye. I knew better than to ask for Bushmills in a joint like this. Various girls stopped to talk to me, but none of them made much of an impression until this skinny girl with a birthmark on her temple and short, dirty blonde hair and the most perfect, pear-shaped ass I'd ever seen asked me if I wanted a dance. So I said all right, and she led me to the back of the room and had me sit down in a chair quite close to the first chair I'd sat in, but, happily, the light in this new location was better. Her name was Chantal, and, like most of the girls who work in these bars — the ones who tell the truth, at least — she was from small-town Quebec. Not that she could have claimed otherwise — her accent gave her away. The music started and she knelt in front of me and leaned her head into my neck. Her breasts were smaller than Valerie's, but at least they were real. We talked a bit. She told me about a friend of hers named Jasmine — she pronounced it Shaz-*meen* — who had just arrived in town and was working here, too, her first night, and would I hire her — Jasmine — for a dance? I told Chantal I didn't have much money with me, and she said the dance she was giving me was free, and I could give the money I was going to give her to Jasmine instead. I said she struck me as a good person, and she said she tried to be, but it was hard when you worked in a place like this. Then she stood up and lifted one leg and laid the back of her ankle on my shoulder, and there were no gold rings down there, and she didn't do any heavy thrusting so I didn't have to tell her to back off. When she removed her leg I did something I shouldn't have: I put my hands on her hips. There are signs all over the place saying NO TOUCHING THE DANCERS! but I guess I just forgot for a moment where I was and who I was with. Chantal gently moved my hands back to the armrests of my chair, but not before a bouncer bellowed at me. We both flinched, and Chantal turned her head and told him it was okay, and after he took a threatening step towards me and glared for a solid fifteen seconds, he went away. She said, "He is new 'ere and ver' rude. He is more *dangereux*, I t'ink, dan any of de customer."

What I'd said about not having much money was true, so when the dance was over I asked Chantal to stay where she was and walked over to one of several ATM machines conveniently situated throughout the club and withdrew two hundred dollars from my chequing account.

I spent a hundred and forty dollars on Chantal — seven more dances. When I told her it was time for me to leave, I gave her another twenty to pass along to Jasmine. She looked me in the eyes, then reached into the little purse she carried and took out a folded piece of paper.

"You might not t'ink so to see me 'ere," she said, "but I am *étudiante*. In Montreal, at one of de *colleges* 'dere." She swept her naked arm towards the other dancers. "'Dis is 'ow I earn my tuition, but I am not *stupide*, eh, and sometime I write a poem? I write in English much better 'dan I talk it. I write dis poem dis afternoon before I come to work. Whenever I write a poem, I give it to my *fah-vor-eet* customer and den I never t'ink about it again. Today you are my *fah-vor-eet* customer." She proffered the piece of paper, and I took it. She glanced to her left and right, then kissed me quickly on the mouth. "I'm next girl on stage," she said. "I would like it if you watch me."

So I stayed. I sat at a small table on the balcony that ran along one wall of the room and watched her routine, for which she dressed up like a skateboarder — baggy pants, sneakers, a halter top, and a bandana. She danced to rap music, which I normally can't abide. Not this night. She was well received by the audience, especially when she did some gymnastics with the fire pole. There was much clapping and whistling, and I felt proud — almost paternal. I felt connected, as if something real had happened between us.

The next night I returned to Gents. At first I couldn't find Chantal. She wasn't near the bar, or up on the balcony. I walked towards the gloomy rear of the room, where the private dances take place. Then I saw her. She was naked and straddling a businessman, whose tie was askew and whose eyes were focused on her breasts. Over his lap, she was slowly lifting and lowering, in a kind of female-superior mock-fuck. She turned her head to pull a few strands of dingy blonde hair from her eyes and looked straight at me. I don't know if she saw me or not, but even though I nodded and smiled and half-raised my hand, she didn't react. She just went back to her business. I turned around and made my way to the bar and ordered a beer. I waited awhile, hoping she would walk by and recognize me. After I finished my beer, I wandered around some more and found her dancing for a young man at a table full of young men. He was a university student probably — cropped hair, fogged-up glasses. She was leaning over him and nuzzling his neck, and he was sending slapstick looks of alarm towards his friends, who were laughing and slapping their knees and high-fiving each other.

When it was Chantal's turn on stage, I sat at the same little table on the balcony as I had the previous night. She was dressed as a skateboarder again. Even from that distance I could see the vacant, glazed look in her eyes.

ah drugs i say
at the end of a working day
i pass the joint to you
where you sit on my sofa
watching videos
do not think it is my custom
to bring home customers
i think it was your mouth
you have a wonderful mouth
my room is down the hall
bring the candle and we will cast
giant shadows against the ceiling
bring the cigarettes
i will not ask you anything
about yourself
when i fall in love
it is only for the evening
the time it takes
to shoot me up
do not think of me
as your lover
tomorrow i will not think
of you at all
close the door
i made this lampshade
this sword
open your mouth

* * *

About a month after the cops raided McCully's and Finn Boyle went berserk on them and got hauled away, things had cooled off enough that Vinnie let it be known through the grapevine that the bookies were welcome to come back, and so the rest of us all moved back, too. Except Finn Boyle. We heard that he was out of jail, but we never saw him again. He just quietly disappeared. Maybe he went back where he came from. Maybe he went to see his kids and his ex. Or maybe he went down to Buffalo, New York, where he told me his sister lived. All I know is he never came back for his cherished black oak walking stick. Of course, he probably doesn't even know where it is. He doesn't know it's under the bar here at McCully's, or that Dexter uses it from time to time to chase away obstreperous drunks, like the guy today, the guy with the scar like a pucker.

I climb down from my stool and walk over to Dale.

"Five across on number eight, please."

Dale shakes his head. "You know what happens when you bet with your heart instead of your head."

I place the money on his tray. "For old times' sake, Dale. For Finn Boyle. Five across on Red Scout."

"Well, you're two for two. I guess you can afford it. *Cinco al ocho.*"

Even though he's ancient and has bandages on all four legs, and even though he bowed a tendon when he was half his present age and has run crooked ever since, and even though some days he's more interested in a leisurely jog than anything resembling a full-out gallop, Red Scout is firing on all cylinders today and rallies from last to first in stirring fashion to win by a length and three-quarters.

Head or heart, I've got the touch today. When the numbers come up, Red Scout pays $18.20, $8, and $4.50. At five across, I collect $76.75. Dale rounds it off to $77. Take off a deuce for the dealer and $15 for the bet and I net $60. Add that to my previous bankroll, and after only three races I'm up a sweet one hundred and seventy-one simoleons, less Anna's fifty.

FOURTH RACE

POST TIME: 2:27 P.M.

(6 FURLONGS.
3- AND 4-YEAR-OLD MAIDENS.
CLAIMING $11,500–12,500.
PURSE $18,800.)

1 DON'T EXPLAIN
2 MARS
3 INFLUENTIAL
4 CAZAVILLE
5 SADSACK MCALPINE
6 TOP MARKS
7 POP-A-WHEELIE
8 ROUGH HOUSE
9 MR. J.M.

Old Gordon, who has been sitting beside me quiet as a mouse all afternoon, has ordered lunch, and Jessy lays it before him. It's the special: beef ribs, ninety cents a piece. There are six on the plate and they're each about a foot long.

He stares at them. "These are sizable."

"Jessy'll have to hose you down after you're finished," I tell him.

"I don't know if I can eat these," he says. "These are

sizable." He turns and looks at me. "Last night I had dinner at Ginger's. Hamburger steak, and it was a nice-size steak. Fried onions, mashed potatoes, peas. A dinner roll with butter. Five dollars and sixty-five cents."

Old Gordon's been a regular at McCully's for the last six months. He's a big man, maybe seventy years old, and always wears a pale blue dress shirt, buttoned at the cuffs and neck. He's a brooder, but always polite when spoken to. His approach to handicapping is straightforward and simple: he only bets favourites. Favourites win about 30 percent of the time, and the short prices they pay don't make up for the 70 percent of the time they lose. So, at the end of the day, Old Gordon, who is basically a two-dollar bettor, is usually down somewhere between ten and twenty dollars. But it doesn't seem to bother him. He always comes back, and he's always even-tempered. I figured he must be on a pension of some kind, so one day I asked him what he'd done for a living:

"My father was a longshoreman and had to lift heavy boxes all the time and it ruined his back, and even when I was still a kid he couldn't work no more and went on the disability. When I was seventeen I dropped out of high school and got a job as a mail sorter at the post office. My father said I was lucky because all I had to lift was letters, plus I had a strong union, so I was set for life. So I liked it for the first while. All I had to do was read the addresses on the envelopes and toss them in the right bin. But after ten years I'd come to hate it. I hated being inside all the time, and it was awful boring, and sometimes I thought if I had to read another address it would kill me. Most of the people I worked with were crazy or they drank, so I started drinking, too. Pretty soon I was sneaking drinks at work, and I was drunk most of the time. The drinking and what my father said about it being a good job kept me where I was. One time, I had a chance to be promoted to shift chief, but I said no. I didn't want the responsibility. They never asked me again. So I kept on sorting mail. I sorted mail for forty-two years. I was six months from retirement when I had what I call my panic attack.

"The way it happened was this: one Saturday the wife sent me to No Frills with a shopping list. I was standing in the household aisle looking for a bottle of shower spray. I found all sorts of other kinds of spray — for soap scum and mildew and so on — but I couldn't find one that was just for cleaning the inside of your shower. Then all of a sudden I just kind of froze up. I couldn't move. I must of stood there an hour before somebody noticed me and called the manager. He took me in his office — he led me by the hand like a child — and give me a cup of coffee, and it was when he give me the cup of coffee I started crying, and I just kept on crying. So he asked me what my phone number was, and I told him, and he called the wife, and she come up in a taxi and found me in his office, and she drove us home and she never even had no licence. That was the first and last time she ever drove a car. And I never drove again neither. And I never went back to work again neither. The doctor wrote a letter for me, and the wife took it to my boss at the post office, and I ended up on the disability, just like my father. Now I'm on this Prozac, and I don't like it one bit, but I've never had no more of those panic attacks. Another good thing is I've cut down on the drinking. I still drink — you know that, you sit right beside me — but not the way I used to. That was eleven years ago when all that happened.

"Nowadays I just come here or I go to the Legion. I've

been a member since 1951, the year I started at the post office, even though I wasn't in the armed forces. My father got a friend of his to sponsor me. I mostly play shuffleboard or listen to the veterans.

"Two years ago the wife lost her mind. I had to put her in a home. She's there now. It don't seem to bother her, but it bothers the hell out of me. I get on the streetcar every morning about eleven and get there in time to help her with her lunch. In the summertime if it's not too hot I'll call for a taxi from the nurses' station and take her back to the house, and we'll sit on the patio, which was my birthday present to her a few years ago. Neighbour's boy laid it for me, and I paid him for the work. Interlocking bricks. Grey, with a pink border, which he thought up. Now when I take her out there she don't even know where she is. I buy baskets of pansies and petunias and what-all and put them out there, but she don't even notice. Like I say, I visit her every day. The staff tell me not to visit so often. That's because sometimes she don't recognize me, and they think it's hard on me. 'Where's Gordon?' she'll say to me. 'I want Gordon.' Well, it *is* hard on me, but I don't have nothing else to do except come down here and play the horses. I'm not a very good gambler, but you know what? I still like to put my two dollars down."

Old Gordon stares at his ribs.

"Want some extra sauce for those?" Jessy asks him.

"I don't know if I can eat these," he says.

The bar is filling up. I turn to my right and Zontar, a short, pot-bellied, thirties-ish accountant with not very much hair is sitting on the stool beside me. "Hi, Mr. Harvey," he says.

"Hey," I say.

Zontar, whose real name is Walter, wears blue jeans with the bottoms turned up and red suspenders over his white T-shirt. Right now he is simultaneously playing the trivia game on TV #2 and studying the songlist in the karaoke catalogue Jessy keeps on the bar. I didn't see him come in, but he always arrives between two and three o'clock. He sees himself as an accomplished, if undiscovered, entertainer, and at four o'clock when the karaoke begins, he wants to be ready for the supper crowd. As he will be the first to tell you, his specialties are Stevie Wonder and Marvin Gaye. Zontar is his self-appointed trivia game name — another pursuit he takes very seriously. Whenever TV #2 says ROAD SCHOLAR: ZONTAR!!!, I pat him on the shoulder. "All right, Zontar!" I'll say. "The main man."

The themes for the game he's playing right now are WORLD LEADERS, MOVIES, RIVERS, ROYALTY, and BASEBALL. I rarely play the game myself, but I don't mind helping if I'm asked.

The question on the screen reads, IN WHICH OF HIS MOVIES DOES PAUL NEWMAN PLAY "SULLY," A "LIKEABLE WORKING-CLASS STIFF WHO'S MADE A LIFETIME OF BAD DECISIONS"?

A) QUINTET

B) POCKET MONEY

C) SOMETIMES A GREAT NOTION

D) NOBODY'S FOOL

E) THE VERDICT

Zontar says, "Um, Mr. Harvey, could you —"

"D," I tell him.

Zontar hits the button on his console.

"Nice little flick," I add. "I'm guessing it was made about ten years ago."

Zontar says, "I was sure I'd seen all Paul Newman's films, but that title doesn't ring a bell."

"It's set in upstate New York," I tell him. "He plays this ageing jack-of-all-trades sort of a guy, who lives in a furnished room."

Zontar shakes his head. "Doesn't ring a bell."

"He hasn't seen his family in years, and his only friends are his elderly landlady and the village idiot. Jessica Tandy plays the elderly landlady. It was her last movie before she died."

Zontar scratches his head. "Nope, I'm afraid —"

"And Sully's son, who's having marital problems, comes to visit, and ends up working with him."

"With Paul Newman?"

"With Sully, the Paul Newman character, doing construction."

"I tell you, I'm drawing a complete blank here."

"And Melanie Griffith and Bruce Willis are in it, too. They play a married couple, and Bruce owns a construction company, and Melanie's got a crush on Paul —"

"Oh, wait a minute, wait a minute, I remember now. That's the one where you get to see Melanie Griffith's tits, right?"

"Right, but only for fraction of a —"

"And there's a poker game towards the end of the film, and there's this naked girl sitting next to Bruce Willis, and you get to see her tits, too?"

"That's right."

"And one's bigger than the other?"

"That, I couldn't tell you."

"Oh yes, one's bigger than the other." Zontar smiles happily up at TV #2, ready for the next question. "I knew I'd seen all his films."

The photo of eight-year-old Shannon Brown appears on TV #3. She's been missing since 1996, and a second picture, computer-enhanced, shows what she might look like today, at sixteen. If they're right, and if she's still alive, she's numbingly beautiful. She's just one of many missing children who get a thirty-second spot on TV #3, but she's the one who always catches my attention. Something in her eyes, I guess, when the photo was taken. She looks happy. She has expectations. She trusts whoever is taking the picture. I first noticed her three or four weeks ago. She's from Beaverton, a small town about seventy miles north of here. According to the information on the screen, she has blonde hair and blue eyes. You can't really tell from the pictures, which are black and white. They figure she's around five feet and a hundred pounds. Tiny thing. Of course, what she more than likely is, is a small, undiscovered skeleton half-buried in a road allowance somewhere outside of Beaverton. But I could be wrong. Maybe her parents split up and one of them abducted her. There's no information about the circumstances of her disappearance.

Sometimes I think I'm the only person in here who pays any attention to the missing children. The only time anyone else concentrates on TV #3 is when a sweating and scantily-clad young woman is doing squat thrusts. But maybe they've got the right idea. While they're ogling and making jerk-off gestures over what still lives and breathes, I'm pining over the image of an eight-year-old girl who I'm guessing was raped and murdered so long ago that I was still working and functional at the time it happened.

"Mr. Harvey," Dexter says, "phone's for you."

I get off my stool and squeeze between the bar and the island, down to where the phone is, behind the cash register, next to the bags of potato chips.

"Hello," I say.

"Priam Harvey?" a man's voice says.

"The same."

"Pry, you old son of a gun," the voice says, "I've been trying to track you down for two days!"

The voice is familiar, but I can't quite place it. "Who is this?"

"Kelvin Chan!"

"Kelvin Chan, you old piece of dog meat, how the hell are you?" I've known Kelvin for a long time, maybe twenty years. He's what you call a public trainer, which means he trains horses for anyone who will hire him — as opposed to training exclusively for one stable. Our careers followed pretty much parallel paths, and many a night we found ourselves in the same bar near the same track in the same town — mostly Fort Erie and Montreal and Toronto. As a matter of fact, he and I were sitting at the same table at the Horsemen's Benevolent and Protective Association Ball last New Year's Eve when I rediscovered long-legged Anna, my current inamorata. I remember because Kelvin, who's half-Chinese and shaped like a miniature sumo wrestler, was wearing a pink tuxedo. His cummerbund was pink, his top hat was pink, even his shoes were pink. Kelvin's never had very good horses, but he's a flashy dresser. And he's an all-round good guy. Give-you-the-shirt-off-his-back type of guy. He had a decent little colt named Ebony Tree I did a piece on a few years ago. You don't see pure black thoroughbreds very often, but Ebony Tree was one.

"I'm good, I'm good," he says, "but how are *you*? Getting by?"

"Hand to mouth," I tell him.

"Well, that's why I've been trying to get in touch with you. I heard you got fired —"

"That was a year ago."

"Really? That long? Because I was thinking maybe I could steer some business your way."

"I'm okay for money, if that's what you're thinking. It's not like I'm panhandling or sleeping in the park. Not yet anyway. If I don't do anything reckless, I can last another month or two."

"Still gambling, Pry?"

I look at the little bags of potato chips arrayed vertically in front of me, as if on a ladder. "Small wagers here and there, judiciously placed."

"You betting with the books?"

"Yes, Dale's currently in residence. You know Dale."

"Yes, I know Dale, but you're not going to make a fortune off him, are you? How big a bet will he take?"

"Couple hundred."

"That's not much. And he probably won't pay more than twenty to one, is that fair to say?"

"I'm not trying to make a fortune here, just trying to get by."

"Well, like I say, that's why I'm calling. I thought maybe you could use a little scratch."

"I'm listening."

"My barn hasn't been doing all that great lately. You know how it goes, you make a couple of bad claims, people think you've lost your touch. So, I got to thinking maybe some publicity couldn't hurt —"

"You know I'm not writing anymore —"

"No, no, no, not like one of those stories you used to write for the magazines. What I want you to do — if you're interested — is write me some advertising."

"Advertising?"

"Yes, like in the *Form*. You know: 'Kelvin Chan has a public stable, he's been in the business for, what, twenty years, he's honest and he's looking for customers, or clients, or whatever.' Something like that."

"You don't need me. Just phone up the *Form* and tell them what information you want included. They'll print up the ad for you. Ask for Dick Styles. Run it in *Sport of Kings*, too. Ask for Marsha. If a guy named Reed answers, don't mention my name. Or better yet, hang up immediately."

"But I want you to write it for me," Kelvin says. "There's fifty bucks in it for you."

Fifty bucks. During my long and slow decline into moral and professional bankruptcy, I would have written anything for fifty bucks. "No," I say. "I appreciate the offer, I really do, but my writing days are over. On the other hand, if you had a horse you could recommend, that'd be different, that's the sort of help I'd happily accept."

There's a pause. "Well, okay, I've got one in today. Matter of fact, she's the only decent horse I've got."

"Really?" I say, straightening slightly. "Which race?"

"The stake, no less."

"You're kidding me."

"I am not kidding you. And furthermore, she's golden. She's only run four times, but won three of them. I tell you what, Pry, she's freaky fast."

"You like her that much?"

"I don't like her, I *love* her."

"What's her name?"

"Off by Heart."

"Never heard of her. Why haven't I heard of her?"

"She's been down in Philadelphia. I just shipped her up. I've been keeping her a secret, but listen, take it easy on her, and don't go broadcasting it around."

"I hear you."

"And hold some back, just in case she snaps a fetlock or something. The jock falls off."

"You're a good man, Kelvin."

"Fifty across, something like that."

"I hear you. Thanks."

"Take it to the bank, man."

"All right," I laugh, "I will."

"You sure you can't help me out? If it's the money, tell me what you want. Seventy-five?"

"It's not the money. I'd help you if I could, but writing and I have gone our separate ways. I can't even write a shopping list."

"Well, let me know if you change your mind."

"I will."

"Listen, I got to get going. I got a stiff to saddle in the fourth —"

"The fourth? That's right now. Where are you?"

"In the saddling enclosure."

"What's the name of this stiff?"

"Top Marks, but lay off him, Pry, he's a maiden, and he's likely to die a maiden. He couldn't beat *me* at six furlongs."

I hang up, squeeze my way back to my stool, sit down, light a cigarette, and turn back to the *Form*. I haven't even looked at the fourth yet, but before I do I'll just flip ahead to the ninth and circle Kelvin's filly. Off by Heart. Not a squished name. A properly spaced three-word name. Off. By. Heart.

"Hey, Mr. Harvey."

Jesus, it's like Grand Central in here. I look to my right and Zontar's gone and Panther's taken his place.

"Where'd Zontar get to?" I ask.

"He went to talk to the karaoke guy. He said I could sit here."

"Fine," I say, and quickly turn my attention back to the *Form.* I've got ten minutes till post time.

But I can't concentrate. I can never concentrate when Panther's around. I listen as he orders a Molson Canadian, the beer of the masses. I listen to the small talk he makes with Dexter. I wait for him to speak to me again, as I know he will.

Panther is in no way pantherish. It's my sense of irony that makes me call him Panther. He is neither black nor ferocious. He is, in fact, quasi-intellectual, but he's the kind of quasi-intellectual who enjoys slumming. He might call it something else — integrating, research, being one with the people — but what he's really doing is slumming. That white collar he wears to work on weekdays at whatever ivory tower employs him — I make it a point not to ask him about his personal life — turns blue in his spare time when he comes down here to rub elbows with the great unwashed. He seems to want my approval — of his bets, of his questions, of his life, I suppose — though I can't figure out why he would want the approval of an alcoholic ex-racetrack journalist who lives in a furnished room in a rundown building whose tenants, almost without exception, are, like him, hopeless drunks. He's the guy with the healthy career. Wife and two kids and a bungalow in the 'burbs. Well, I don't know that for a fact — like I say, I make a point not to ask.

I call him Panther for two reasons: one, because he wears an old black hockey jacket with the word PANTHERS stitched in red across the shoulder blades; and two, to let him know that I don't like him enough to learn his real name. The jacket could be his, I suppose, or his teenaged son's, if he has one, or plunder from a yard sale. Whatever, he looks ridiculous in it — skinny and balding and bespectacled as he is.

I think the reason he likes to talk to me is because I can keep up with him.

"Who do you like?"

My head is drawn upward from the *Form* like a bucket on a rope. Ineluctably. "We're talking maidens here, Panther. Non-winners in their lifetimes. Horses whose owners are quickly giving up on them. Whatever I like or don't like is more than usually subject to racing luck, jockey competence, and equine whimsy."

He smiles in his clever way. "You didn't answer my question."

To mess him up I could say Pop-a-Wheelie, which boasts not only an unbettably bad name but also an unbelievably bad effort in his last race — forty-five lengths off the winner. Or I could give him Kelvin's stiff, another sure loser. But I can't do it. In certain matters I have integrity. Being asked which horse I like is one of them.

"Cazaville," I say.

The first time I met Panther, a couple of months ago, he came up behind my stool, put his hand on my shoulder like we were old pals and said, "You're Priam Harvey. One of the twins just told me. You write for *Sport of Kings*." Maybe he thought he was sharing information that might prove useful to me. Maybe he thought I would be impressed by his association with the twins, an association he has still not learned will stunt, not nurture, his popularity amongst the McCully's regulars.

"Correction," I said. "I *used* to write for *Sport of Kings*."

He laughed, waving my words away. "I wouldn't mind working there," he said.

"You wouldn't? Well, maybe you should apply for a job. Ask for a fellow called Reed. Tell him you're a friend of mine."

His smile dissolved. "You really don't work there anymore?"

"That's what I'm telling you, friend."

"Since when?"

"Coming up on a year. Fired me, the bastards did." I was in my cups.

"I'm sorry. I didn't know. I hadn't seen your name recently, but I figured ... I don't know what I figured. Listen, I'm really sorry."

I shrugged my shoulders. "Doesn't matter. I wrote a column nobody read. It was just sugar on the pill. My job was to help make a corrupt industry look classy, and that's what I did. For thirty-one years. Now I have a new job." I raised my glass.

"I remember a piece you wrote about some guy who only had one horse, and how things had gone badly for him and he was leaving to go back home somewhere out west with his pick-up truck and his trailer and his old gelding and all his earthly possessions. That was a beautiful piece."

I looked at him. He had recalled one of the few good columns I managed to write in the last year or two of my career. One of the half-dozen pieces some owner or trainer or jockey's agent hadn't bribed me into writing with fifty dollars or a bottle of whiskey.

"Echo Lake," I said.

"Beg your pardon?"

"Name of the horse. Echo Lake. Can't remember the guy's name. Brian something."

There was a silence, then Panther said, "I write, too."

I hate it when people tell me they write. It's like they expect me to get down on my knees in front of them. Like they expect a hush to fall over the room and a saintly glow to gather around their heads. "Really," I said.

"Actually, I've published two books. Poetry." He smiled at me.

"Congratulations." I turned back around.

"Sorry. Just thought you might be interested."

Studying my beer, I said, "I'm not interested. I'm here to have a few drinks and lose a few bucks. I'm not one of your colourful characters or an anecdote for one of your I've-been-everywhere poems. By the way, I've read more poetry, *memorized* more poetry than you'll ever read. Who's your favourite poet?"

He pulled in his chin. "Well, I'd have to think about it —"

"Come on, who's your favourite poet?"

He cleared his throat. "I guess I'd have to say Frost."

"I should have known. Poet of the people. Mind you, he wasn't a very nice man, was he? Mean son of a bitch, despite the grandfatherly exterior. Half his children committed suicide, but I'm sure you already know that. What's your favourite poem?"

"By Frost?"

"Who are we talking about, Rod McKuen?"

"I thought maybe you meant my favourite poem of all time. Just because Frost is my favourite poet doesn't necessarily mean —"

"Oh for fucksake, what's your favourite poem by Robert Frost?"

"'Out, out —'"

My turn to smile. "'And they, since they were not the one dead, turned to their affairs.'"

He nodded. "I'm impressed."

I shake my head. "Not my intention to impress. Do you make your living as a poet?"

"I don't refer to myself as a poet. Frost said it was a praise-word he wasn't worthy of, and if Frost felt that *he* wasn't worthy —"

"Very noble of you. So how *do* you make your living?"

He paused to catch his breath. "I teach —"

"Ah, yes, of course."

"— English lit and creative writing at a community college."

"Hence the two books of poetry."

He nodded.

"Vanity press, I presume."

"No, they're not vanity press. Why are you so hostile?"

"Do you use 'Out, out —' when you're teaching?"

"Yes, as a matter of fact. And 'Death of the Hired Man' and 'Birches' and 'Mending Wall.'"

"What about 'Stopping by Woods' and 'The Road not Taken'?"

"I teach twenty-year-olds, Mr. Harvey, not sixth graders."

* * *

Afterward, I wondered why I had been so hard on him. He was no worse than a lot of other casual acquaintances I make sitting in bars. In fact, he had a lot more to offer than most. Hell, I hadn't talked poetry with anyone in years. But, as drinkers are wont to do, I was prepared to forget the whole encounter: last night's disagreement being nothing more than a blur the next morning. In this case, however, when the next morning came I not only remembered meeting Panther and the conversation we'd had, I knew why he'd got my back up.

After I graduated from high school, I worked at the track for a couple of years as a groom, and then I got a job at the *Daily Racing Form*, and after a year of being a file clerk, I was sent to Blue Bonnets Race Track in Montreal to work in the press box. I was mostly just a gofer, but whenever the regular man was too drunk to write his column — which was fairly often — I'd do it for him under his byline. My editor noticed the change in style when I filled in. He said my columns read like essays. But he liked me. "Next time Pierre's too drunk to file," he wired me from Toronto, "use your own name. And keep your paragraphs to one sentence. Our readers like lots of white space and plenty of dialogue."

I had toyed with the idea of becoming a high school teacher, but instead of going to university to pursue a teaching degree, I asked my editor if he could keep me employed year-round. He said he could but I'd be better off teaching, doing a job that had a positive impact on people's lives instead of working in an industry that almost always had a negative impact. "You're going to be a wage-earner for the next thirty-five years," I remember him saying. "How do you want to spend that time — helping people to realize their potential or helping to ruin them?"

It was a big admission for him to make — he was basically saying he'd wasted his own career years — but he did add that if I really wanted him to, he would give me the southern circuit for the winter. The southern circuit was all B-tracks. Ellis Park in Kentucky, Evangeline Downs in Louisiana, Sunshine Park in Florida. Places like that. B-tracks are like B-movies. Movies with titles like *Cellblock Sisters* or *Blood Orgy of the She-Devils*. They're cheerfully second-rate. B-tracks are like the B-side on the old forty-fives I used to listen to when I was a kid. Ray Charles, my first musical influence, recorded "Drown in My Own Tears" as an A-side. It reached #1 on the Billboard R&B charts in 1956. Nobody remembers the B-side, a non-starter called "Mary Ann." There are exceptions to the rule, of course, but the B-side was almost always second-rate. And the same can be said for B-tracks. Broken-down horses. Bribable jockeys. Greedy owners. Unscrupulous trainers.

Drunken journalists.

Anyway, I ignored my editor's advice about doing something useful with my life, took him up on his offer, and headed south to cover the B-tracks. And that, essentially, is the story of my life.

While I was still working in Montreal I had a girl living with me and what happened with her should have shown me what my future was going to be like, but it seems that whenever my important life lessons show up I'm either too drunk to pay them any attention or just plain oblivious to what's going on.

It was night racing, and Sylvie used to walk over about the seventh race from this little apartment we had on rue Jean Talon and wait for me to come down from the press box when I was finished working. Then we'd go over to one of the bars on Decarie where the horsemen drank. In fact, that's where we met — in one of those bars. But she wasn't there to drink and she wasn't waiting tables. No, like Chantal, Sylvie — pronounced Syl-*vee*, if you knew what was good for you — was a stripper. She had a small, sculpted head, and straight black hair to her shoulders. She was slim, clear-complected — she wore hardly any makeup — and direct. Shortly after she moved in with me, I found her a job in a bank. She didn't make as much money as she did stripping, but I was earning enough to supplement her, and besides, I was sick of watching drunks stuffing bills into her G-string.

Everything was going beautifully — I had a job and a girl and money in my pocket — until one night when a horse named Wise Old Bird broke down in front of the grandstand. It was the last race of the card. With about a hundred yards to go, Wise Old Bird had the race sewn up. Johnnie Dale Bacon was the jockey. But the horse took a bad step, and Johnnie Dale had to pull him up just short of the wire. As the rest of the field went by, people in the grandstand who'd backed Wise Old Bird hooted and booed. When the dust settled, Wise Old Bird was standing in the middle of the track as still as a monument, and Johnnie Dale had dismounted and was standing at his head, holding the reins. A groom hopped over the rail, took the reins from Johnnie Dale, and tried to lead the horse back to the barn. From the press box, I was watching the whole thing through my binoculars, and I followed Johnnie Dale as he walked away. Then I panned along to where Sylvie usually met me by the little booth where the Clerk of Scales weighed the jockeys, and there she was, watching it all, hands to her mouth.

Despite his efforts, the groom couldn't get Wise Old Bird to move. Wise Old Bird was one of my favourite horses at Blue Bonnets. I'd followed him for years, going back to when he was a young turf prospect, imported from England. Now he was just another has-been, running for peanuts. But he was a classy sort, and I hated to see him break down.

And there was Sylvie watching it all. Watching Wise Old Bird raise his hoof — it was the right fore — to relieve the pressure on the fracture, then when the pain subsided a bit, lower it to the track and put his weight back on it. As his ears pricked back with pain, he lifted the damaged hoof again, his ears settled back forward, he calmed down, lowered the hoof again, and put his weight back on it. Horses aren't as smart as dogs: they don't always know when to favour an injured limb. So the pain shot back through him, the ears pricked back, he lifted the hoof. The pain subsided, he lowered the hoof. The whole process repeated itself three or four times a minute for the ten minutes it took the horse ambulance to get to him. By which point, every time the old boy lowered his hoof it went straight out to the side and his weight was all on the bottom of his cannon bone, so that when he jerked his knee up again there was only a shred of hide holding his dangling hoof to the leg.

By the time I got down from the press box, Sylvie was weeping into her handkerchief. I tried to lead her away, but she wouldn't go. The vet couldn't get the horse up the ramp to the ambulance, so two men held a large blanket in such a way that the few spectators who were still hanging around the grandstand to watch this tragedy unfold couldn't see the vet administer the lethal injection. We did, however, see the horse's head and neck as he reared up in his death throes, and we did see the two men holding the blanket scramble to avoid the thrashing hooves as Wise Old Bird pitched forward into the dirt.

After that, Sylvie wouldn't come to the track anymore. When the meet ended in late August, she gave me an ultimatum: horse racing or her. Well, I loved her, I truly did, but I loved the track more, so we went our separate ways. Except for Barbara, Sylvie is the only woman I ever loved. I never loved my son's mother — her name was Eula, and I was only with her for a few weeks — and as far as Anna is concerned, I don't love her even remotely, and she doesn't love me. I may refer to her as my inamorata, but it's not as if we live together or share a bank account. I'm just one of many sources of entertainment for her. One of these days she'll lose interest and vanish from my life like yesterday's news.

So there you have it. That's why Panther got my back up. Because he's a teacher and I'm not. Because his profession is important and mine isn't. Because if I'd ended up in a classroom instead of a press box, I might have married the girl I loved, and I might have become a productive member of society and had a positive impact on the lives of my students. Alumni would have visited me in the evenings, like Mr. Chips in the old movie, and we'd drink tea and discuss poetry. As it is, my only regular visitors are Tommy Belyea when he needs to get away from his mother for a while, and Mrs. Belyea herself, who doesn't know what planet she's on.

"Cazaville?" Panther says. "Can he get the distance?"

"They're only going six, Panther. It's not like they're going a route of ground. But he'll be on the engine, so it all depends how the jockey rates him. He might use him up early."

"How are you going to bet him?"

"I'm not going to bet him."

"But you said you liked him."

"Just because I like a horse doesn't mean I'm going to bet him."

"But why won't you bet?"

"Because you make me nuts, that's why. Because I can't focus on my handicapping with you sitting beside me asking a lot of fool questions. So I think I'll give this race a pass. It's safer."

Panther frowns. "I didn't think you were a 'safer' sort of guy." He gets down from his stool and heads off in Dale's direction.

One afternoon, about a month ago, we were sitting here at the bar and Panther was going on about his teaching job at the community college, and he referred to his colleagues.

"Your what?" I said.

"My colleagues."

"You mean the people you work with."

"Yes, of course I mean the people I work with."

"Well," I said, "maybe that's what you should call them: 'the people I work with.'" I pointed at the bottle of Canadian nestled in his right hand. "You drink the workingman's beer. You wear a hockey jacket. If you want to come across blue collar, talk blue collar. Talk the talk, Panther."

"'Colleagues' is a perfectly good word, Mr. Harvey. I'm sure it's part of your vocabulary."

"Not in this bar."

"Why not?"

"Because it has attitude. It says, 'Look at me, I went to university.'"

He stared at me for a good ten seconds, then got off his

stool — without another word, that was the best part — and walked out of the bar. Didn't see him for two weeks.

Now, as I watch him walking towards Dale to place his bet, I call out, "Don't bet heavy. Bet light — place or show — and don't say I didn't warn you."

On my left, Old Gordon, covered in rib grease, nudges me with an elbow and mumbles, "Look at that." On TV #3 the bronzed, bikini-clad young woman I saw before the first race is back again, working out on some kind of machine that requires her to kneel and lift, kneel and lift, while a muscle-bound moron crouching behind her barks, "Harder, Melissa! Five more. Harder now! You can do it! Four more!"

Old Gordon and I watch quietly until Panther returns.

"Well, I hope you're right," he says. "I bet ten to win on him."

"On Cazaville?"

"Isn't that who you told me?"

"I told you he was a pace setter who's likely to fade and I told you to bet light. That's what I told you."

"You said you liked him."

"Panther, there are two fundamental skills you have to master before you can become a successful horseplayer: one, you have to pick the right horse, and two, you have to know how to bet him. In this case, I told you I wasn't going to bet him — obviously because I don't have much confidence in him — but if *you* were going to, to bet place or show."

Even though I don't have a bet down, I watch the race anyway. You never know what you'll see that might prove useful in the future. Horses rounding into form. Horses who finish fourth or fifth today, but show some late kick. Horses who'll win next time.

Cazaville scoots out to an early lead. He's in front by five at the half. Beside me Panther's screaming like an idiot, "Come *on*, Cazaville! Come *on*, Cazaville!" At the head of the lane Cazaville's head begins to bobble, and I know he's done. But Panther's still screaming. I have to stick my fingers in my ears until it becomes clear even to him that his horse is finished. By the time the poor nag staggers across the finish line, he's a distant third. Kelvin's horse, Top Marks, finishes last. The rail horse, a first time starter named Don't Explain, makes a late but determined charge to get up for second. Maybe the trainer will stretch him out next time. Seven furlongs maybe. Definitely one to watch.

FIFTH RACE

(1 Mile. Turf.
Fillies and Mares, 4-Year-Olds and Up.
Allowances.
Purse $64,000.)

1 Nun
2 Ruthless [GB]
3 Elmer's Caroline
4 Starrystarrynight
5 Cosmetic
6 The Lorelei [Ire]
7 Guirlande [Fr]
8 Laughing Nancy
9 Heaven on Earth

I'm just thinking how satisfying it is to show restraint, **to** have laid off a race I would have lost, how it's just as good as winning, really, when I spy Mrs. Belyea standing in a diminishing ray of sunlight at the entrance, the door slowly closing behind her. She's looking for Tommy, no doubt, but when her sight falls on me, she lights up, and her worried expression changes to pure joy. Too bad the only person happy to see me these days is mentally ill. She's applied a

Surrey Libraries City Centre Branch

Title: Twelve trees /
ID: 39090024957751
Due: 15/May/2013

Total items: 1
24/Apr/2013

For Renewals, Due dates, Holds & Fines check
your account online at:
www.surreylibraries.ca
or call: 604-502-6333
Thank you for using the
3M Selfcheck System.

fresh jag of lipstick to her mouth, and her bleached blonde hair is completely out of control. She's still wearing the scarlet jogging suit, and she's smoking a cigarette. She looks like Carol Channing.

On my right, Panther is still crying over Cazaville as I get down from my stool, *Form* in hand, and take a few steps towards Mrs. Belyea.

"Mr. Harvey," she says, "how nice to see you. I just dropped by because I was wondering if by any chance you had seen my Tommy. He was supposed to be home for supper an hour ago."

"No, Mrs. Belyea, I haven't seen Tommy, but" — and I point towards the bar — "do you see that nice-looking fellow in the black hockey jacket sitting next to where I sit?"

"The one that says Panthers?"

"That's right. Well, not ten minutes ago he was telling me he saw Tommy at work, and that Tommy said to tell you he'll be home between eight and nine. Go ahead and sit on my stool, Mrs. Belyea, he'll tell you all about it."

"Why, thank you, Mr. Harvey. You are such a gentleman."

I head for the men's room — the only way I'm going to find enough solitude to handicap the fifth is to lock myself in a cubicle — but before I'm even halfway across the dance floor Zontar calls from the bar, "Mr. Harvey, help!"

I look up at TV #2.

THE ACADEMY AWARD-WINNING FILM *ROUND MIDNIGHT* (1986) STARRED WHAT REAL-LIFE JAZZ MUSICIAN?

A) WYNTON MARSALIS

B) DEXTER GORDON

C) GERRY MULLIGAN

D) PHIL WOODS

E) BRANFORD MARSALIS

"Quick, I'm already losing points —"

"B," I tell him, and he punches the keyboard.

In the men's room I sit down in the cubicle and fold the *Form* to the fifth race: a mile on the turf for fillies and mares. Right away, I eliminate the two and eight because they don't show much in the way of recent form. I eliminate the one because she hasn't started since May. I eliminate the three because she's never run on grass before, and her workouts don't impress. And I eliminate the four and the seven because they don't fit the distance. That leaves the five and six, Cosmetic and The Lorelei. They both come from good stables, both their trainers are hot, their jockeys are among the best, they've faced each other twice this year under similar conditions and each has beaten the other. So what separates them? Just one thing: The Lorelei is coming out of a stakes race in which she finished third to the good mare Scullery Maid. In other words, she's dropping in class, running with easier. Cosmetic, on the other hand, is coming off a tough, fully extended, front-end, half-length victory just ten days ago against competition similar to what she's facing today. She'll be the chalk because she won last time out, but I think she'll tire. The Lorelei is the one to beat.

Before I stand up I notice some graffiti staring me straight in the face from the back of the cubicle door. JESSY BLOWS, it reads. Some disgruntled drunk, no doubt, who swung and missed.

I splash some water on my face, dry myself with a handful of paper towel, and re-enter the smoke and noise of the bar. Perched on my stool, Mrs. Belyea has her right arm linked through Panther's left. Panther looks like a trapped rabbit. Jessy has given Mrs. Belyea a drink, something tall and strawberry-coloured, and it has a stick of celery and a green umbrella sticking out of it. I make my way over to Dale, who says, as I approach, "Skip the last one?"

"Just as well. Horse I liked was up the track."

"Lucky man," he says. "You're a lucky man. Lucky when you bet, lucky when you don't. Lucky all the time."

"It's not luck, Dale, it's horses for courses."

"Know when to hold 'em ..."

"Exactly."

"Unlike your young friend over there," he says, and nods towards the bar.

"Maybe he's lucky in love," I say. "Mrs. Belyea seems to have taken a shine."

Dale shakes his head. "*Es un mundo loco.*"

"There's another reason I didn't bet the last race, Dale." I pause for effect.

"And what could that be?"

"I was afraid I was being too hard on you this afternoon."

Dale smiles. "Not to worry. Several of my other parishioners — among them the twins, you'll be happy to hear — have made generous contributions to the collection plate."

"Fine, then I hope you'll accept a wager of twenty across on the six in the fifth."

Dale compresses his lips. "No problem. Twenty across on six in five. Duly noted."

I make my way back to the bar where Mrs. Belyea says, "Oh Mr. Harvey, I've just had the most pleasant conversation with this nice young man. I'm sorry, what is your name again?"

Panther sends a nasty glance my way, then turns to Mrs. Belyea. "Chris," he says.

"Chris?" I laugh. "Chris? And here I've been calling you Panther."

"But he says he doesn't know my Tommy. I thought you said he saw my Tommy at work."

I'm scanning my brain for a clever reply when who should appear in the doorway of the bar but the prodigal son himself. "Mrs. Belyea," I say, "look who's here."

As she turns, Tommy shuffles towards us. Tommy's over six feet, but his shoulders slump and his head hangs. He stops in front of me, eyes fixed on the floor.

"You're home early," I say.

"Landlord phoned me at work," he mumbles. "I left him my work number, just in case, and sure enough he phones me and tells me she's been wandering all over the neighbourhood. So I came home early, which means I'll probably get fired over it. She been bothering you?"

"Not at all, Tommy. She's an asset to the abbey."

"How long she been here?"

"Fifteen minutes, maybe twenty."

"I've been looking all over for her. The parkette, the IGA, the fire hall."

"The fire hall?" Panther says.

Tommy raises his head and regards Panther with suspicion.

"It's okay," I say. "This is Chris. Or you can call him Panther, if you prefer. Panther's his street name."

Tommy lowers his head again and addresses Panther's knees: "She likes to watch them wash their trucks."

Dexter, having spotted the drink in front of Mrs. Belyea, comes over and says, pointedly, "Mr. Harvey," and I say,

"It's time to go, Mrs. Belyea. Suck up that evil concoction, and Tommy'll take you home."

"But Mr. Harvey, this isn't Tommy. This is my other boy."

Tommy says, "Mom, please, for crying out loud."

She leans close to my ear and whispers, "He likes to call himself Tommy, too."

I take her hand and help her down from the stool. "Little Tommy's at home, Mrs. Belyea. Big Tommy will take you there now."

"Thank you for your help, Mr. Harvey," she says. "John and I were worried sick."

Back on my stool, I watch Tommy follow his mother's dignified passage towards the exit. No sooner has the door swung to behind them than it swings sharply open again, and in comes the man with the scar on his face — the man Dexter kicked out of the bar before the first race.

"He's back," I say to Dexter.

"Who?"

"The guy that ordered the Tequila Sunrise. What did he call himself? Short Eyes? He started getting belligerent, so you hoofed him."

As Dexter looks up from behind the bar, his eyes narrow. "Who's that with him?"

An oafish man with orange hair sprouting out of his head like a Chia Pet swaggers in behind the scar-faced man. They're both wearing big smiles like they own the place. The oafish man has his hands in the pockets of his navy blue trench coat, which is buttoned and belted.

The scar-faced man leans one arm on the island, only inches from where the twins are standing. They dart nervous looks at each other and slide farther along.

The oafish man pushes himself up to the bar between

Old Gordon and me. His head is huge and his shoulders are narrow and he smells like garbage.

"You the nigger?" he says to Dexter.

Everything stops. The chatter at the bar, the clink of glasses. Everyone looks at Dexter, who is standing stock-still behind the bar. All you can hear is the jukebox.

"I said, you the nigger?"

Dexter's eyes flash. I've seen them do that once before when a drunk he'd cut off used a racial slur. Dexter glances quickly to his left and down, where Finn Boyle's walking stick lies hidden under the bar. He says nothing.

I feel trapped, not only by the oafish man's terrible odour but because he's squeezing himself against me, hemming me in. Then he puts his right arm around my shoulders and his left around Old Gordon's. He pulls us both towards him, presses his mouth against my ear, and, as if he were speaking to a child, says to me, "Nigger won't talk!" He leans his cheek against mine, clears his throat — I can feel the vibration through our cheeks — tilts his head back, and horks a green glob of sputum across the bar. It hits the door of the microwave and sticks to it like a snail. He says to me, "That's the nigger came at my friend with a crutch." He turns slowly towards Old Gordon, then slowly back to me. "Right?" He clears his throat again, and a second missile rattles the liquor bottles lined up in tiers behind the bar. "Well, well," the man says, tightening his grip on my shoulder, "what should we do? Nigger's too scared to talk to me, and I want to be absolutely sure he hears what I'm saying, so I need you boys to pass along a little message." Then his voice changes from mock-childish to deadly serious. "Tell him nobody comes at my friend with a crutch, 'specially not a black fuck like him." He slides his hand from my shoulder towards my neck and digs his fingertips into the meat above my collar bone. "Go on, tell him."

"You're hurting me," I say, wincing.

"Go on, tell him what I said." His grip tightens. "You hear me? *Tell him*."

I don't know what Old Gordon's doing, but I'm watching my hands shaking in my lap. "Maybe you don't hear what I'm telling you," the oafish man says. "Maybe you're deaf. Is that it? You deaf?"

"No, I'm —"

"Then listen up and listen good. Look at me and say, 'Yes, sir, I'll pass along your message to the nigger coward.'"

I sneak a glance at Old Gordon. Head down, beef rib in one hand. His shoulders are heaving. Is he crying?

I look up at the man. His pale grey eyes are cold and empty. Dead eyes of a killer.

"Yes," I say, my voice unsteady, "I'll pass along the message."

He squeezes tighter. "To the nigger coward. Say it: 'To the nigger coward.'"

I swallow. "Is this really necessary?"

He moves his hand to the back of my neck and squeezes.

I yell.

"Say it, old man: 'To the nigger coward.'"

I close my eyes. I'm seeing stars. My heart's in my throat, jumping. "To the nigger coward," I mumble.

"Louder."

"To the nigger coward!"

"Good. Now say 'Black fuck behind the bar.' Say it."

"Black fuck behind the bar."

"Louder!"

I open my eyes and see Dexter in front of me. I see the muscles in his jaw working. I look down again. "Black fuck behind the bar."

"Shout it!" His fingers on my neck tighten like a clamp.

"Black fuck behind the bar!"

The man releases my neck and pats me on the back. "Good for you," he says. He leans his head into mine, pushes his mouth against my ear, and whispers, "How do I smell, do I smell good?"

He eases off me. I feel his presence behind me, heavy and menacing, and I feel the weight of his breathing. He says, "Come on, Billy, let's get outta this dump," then calls out, "Bye, everybody! Don't worry, we'll be back real soon. We ain't anywhere close to done with Sambo here!" Two sets of footsteps make their way towards the exit. I listen to the door swing open and shut.

I look at my cigarettes on the bar. Their lead-pony book of matches. My shoulder and my neck and my mind are numb.

The bar is silent except for Old Gordon snivelling, and a voice I recognize as Rod Stewart's. *Oh Maggie I wish I'd never —"*

After a while I exhale and look up. Dexter is looking towards the door.

"I —" My voice sounds falsetto, and I clear my throat. "I'm sorry, Dexter."

"It's okay," he says, still watching the door. "Just a blowhard. I would've jumped him, but I was afraid he'd break your neck in the process."

"Phone 56. Get someone down here."

"Nah, he won't be back. I've seen his type before."

"He *said* he'd be back."

Dexter turns from the door and looks at me and says,

"You're white as a sheet, Mr. Harvey. Do you want a drink? Do you want some of your whiskey?"

"No, thank you." I sit up straighter. I adjust the collar of my shirt. "But give Gordon here a splash. Looks like he could use one. It's on me, Gordon."

Two minutes later I'm in the men's room, vomiting into the wash basin. Up come the bacon and eggs from breakfast, as well as the beer and Bushmills I've had this afternoon. When I straighten up to wash my face and rinse my mouth I see my pallid reflection in the mirror above the basin.

I feel dizzy, so I go inside the cubicle and sit down and rest my head in my hands. I can feel my fingers trembling against my temples and cheekbones. I breathe slowly and heavily. Slowly and deeply and heavily, until the fluttering's gone from my throat.

About eight this morning, well before my first drink of the day, I walked along Queen to Horton, picked up a newspaper at the variety store, went into Ginger's Diner and sat down at one of the booths by the window. I have breakfast at Ginger's about three times a week, and a waitress named Judy usually waits on me. Judy's late-forties maybe, skinny and worn out. The look in her eyes makes you think she's been somebody's doormat for a long time, a sort of defensive look as if to say, What do *you* want from me?

What I invariably want from her is eggs over, extra bacon, and rye toast. But, unlike Dexter, who always knows what I want to drink, or Mario, who always knows what kind of haircut to give me, Judy takes nothing for granted.

This morning I already had my paper open to the sports

pages when I noticed her standing near me with coffee pot in hand.

"Good morning," I said.

"Coffee?" she said.

"What happened to your eye?" One eye was black.

"Walked into a door somebody was opening. Coffee?"

It was black with yellow highlights, and the white on one side of her pupil was bright red. "Yes, please."

She poured me a cup. Then she pulled a pencil from behind her ear and pulled her order pad from the front pocket of her uniform. Her uniform was beige with white trim. "Know what you want?"

"Number two, please."

"How do you want the eggs?"

"Over. And extra bacon, please."

"White or brown, multi-grain or rye?"

"Rye, please."

She started to walk away but I said, "Judy, how long have I been coming here?"

She stopped and looked back at me. "How should I know? Don't you know?"

"About a year."

"So why are you asking me?"

"What do I always order?"

She shrugged. "Eggs over. Extra bacon. Rye toast. So what?"

"What's my name?"

"I have no idea." She turned on her heel and walked towards the kitchen.

I looked at the sports pages, found the entries for today's flats at Caledonia, made mental notes for a few horses, and then turned my attention to the people hurrying by the window on their way to work. The women especially. Sometimes I play a game when I'm in a public place — a restaurant or a subway station — and I have time to kill. I'll pick a number at random — five, say — and I'll imagine that the fifth woman who walks by, whoever she is, whatever she looks like, is my new roommate. It's an amusing game because sometimes the fifth woman turns out to be an old bag lady pushing a shopping cart, and I'll laugh out loud at the prospect. Sometimes it's a younger woman, plain of face, maybe, but a decent sort of person who would be good to live with, and I'll nod to myself and delude myself into thinking that a relationship with this total stranger, who probably already has a family and who has already passed out of sight anyway, is somehow possible. Or sometimes the fifth woman will be a real knock-out, long legs, short skirt, high heels, swinging her hips, her breasts out front like the prow of a ship, and the thoughts I get then are entirely different.

Or sometimes when I'm on the subway I'll pretend that all the people on my car, including me, are marooned on a desert island, we're the only people left on earth after a nuclear holocaust, and I'll look around at all the different types of people — male and female, young and old, short and tall, skinny and fat, white, black, brown, red, yellow, Pakistani, Filipino, Mohawk, Jamaican, Serb, Tamil, Salvadoran, Ecuadorean, Chinese, Ethiopian, Sri Lankan, Vietnamese, Guatemalan, Russian — and I'll scrutinize the women and think about which one I would claim as my wife. I would fashion her a hut of bamboo poles and palm fronds and together we would begin the repopulation of the earth.

I saw a thing on TV the other day. Some woman was

being interviewed about love, and she broke it down into three types. When we're young, she said, lust is the primary manifestation of love. Boys hit puberty and they're hard all the time. They can stick it into anything — a toilet paper roll, a pillow, the palm of their hand — they come instantly, and five minutes later, they're hard again. The second type of love, she went on, is romance. That's where you can't think of anything except the other person. If it's a man thinking about a woman, she's on his mind all the time, whether he's with her or not. This kind of love, the woman said, is caused by a chemical surge in the brain. In other words, it's as instinctive a form of behaviour as that exhibited by penguins or baboons. But it's the most dangerous type of love because it's so intoxicating. We love the feeling of being in love, and we often fall in love with the wrong people just because they walk a certain way, or laugh a certain way, or have a certain type of face, or remind us of someone we once knew. And when a romance dies we look around for someone else to fall in love with, because it feels so good when we're in love — it's the greatest feeling in the world — and it feels so bad when we're not. But those extremes of feeling eventually become too much for us to bear, the woman claimed, and we move into the third phase of love, which for the life of me I can't remember the name of. It's sort of recognizing that instead of chasing after some twenty-five-year-old whose interest in you would disappear after about twenty minutes in a hotel room, you choose the person you're most comfortable with, the one who's really your best friend in the world, the one you're *spiritually* loyal to, the one — perhaps the only one — who will stick by you as you begin that long slow slide into physical and mental decay. The only one who will listen to your nonsense and feed you and organize your pills and change your diapers when you're eighty years old. The woman you really bottom-line love and who, for reasons you have no hope of fathoming, loves you back.

Unfortunately for me, those women are gone. Sylvie would have stayed with me if I'd given up horse racing, and Barbara would have stayed if I'd given up drinking. I've no idea what became of Sylvie, but so far as Barbara is concerned, the cabby honked his horn, she picked up her bags, I stood in the doorway with a drink in my hand, and now she's selling houses to the rich and famous. That's what became of her.

When Judy brought my breakfast she was none too delicate about depositing it in front of me. The plate clattered and the silverware crashed. "What's the matter?" I said.

She put her hands on her hips, and I gave her a quick up and down. Mousy hair pinned up. Loose skin under the chin. Scrawny in general. A little belly on her. Don't know why I paid her any attention at all. Oh, yes I do. At times like this I imagine what Barbara would say: "You paid her attention because she wasn't paying you any. Perverse. Wanting what doesn't want you, turning your back on what does."

I looked up at Judy's gaunt, unlovely face. "What's the matter?" I repeated. "What's wrong?"

She stood there for another ten seconds with her hands on her hips before she said, "Why did you ask me if I knew what your name was?"

I shrugged. "Just trying to be friendly. Just trying to make some sort of basic human contact. Sorry if I —"

"What if I *did* know what your name was, what then?"

I looked down at my eggs. "I, um —"

"Would you ask me out? Would you take me home with you?" she said. "Is that the plan? We'd move in together? You and me and the kids? I've got four kids, in case you're interested."

"Listen, I'm sorry, I didn't —"

"One of them's got ADD and another one's hyperactive. They're both on Ritalin. And my sixteen-year-old daughter's out every night doing God-knows-what. I haven't seen or heard from their father since the last time I got pregnant."

I shook my head. "Really, I'm sorry, I —"

"Or do you just want to sleep with me? Is that it? And throw me away when you're done? Like the guy who gave me this?" She jerked a thumb towards her bruised eye. "You must be pretty desperate if you want to sleep with me."

"Shhh," I said, raising my hands like a man with a gun pointed at his head. I glanced around but there was nobody nearby to pay attention. "I'm sorry, I should never have gotten personal with you. I'm very sorry."

Her eyes were full of hatred. She lifted her chin, turned, and walked away.

I wonder if she ever thinks about me. Barbara, I mean.

I remember a scorching Saturday in July a few months before she left. I was supposed to be out at the track at three o'clock to interview the President of the Jockey Club. About ten in the morning I drove up to White Rose to buy some Ant & Grub Killer. White grubs were destroying the lawn, and Barbara had been after me for weeks to do something about it. My argument was that, as tenants, we weren't responsible for the condition of the lawn, the landlord was. Her argument was that appealing to the landlord was a waste of time, so would I please just do it.

I had Barbara's Belgian shepherd, Benny, with me and I left him in the car while I went into the store. The car — Barbara's burgundy Saturn — was Benny's favourite place in the world. What he hated worst in the world was being left behind. We would hear him whine from the bottom of the stairs as we closed the bedroom door behind us. Or if we left him in the backyard he would stand with his nose pressed into the chainlink and look mournful as we backed out of the driveway. So his favourite place in the world was the car. It was simple dog logic: if he was in the car, he couldn't be left behind.

Inside the store the air conditioning felt great. I browsed for a while, enjoying the coolness. I tried to remember if there were other things I should buy. Eventually all I bought were two bags of Ant & Grub.

When I went back outside the heat just about knocked me over. As I walked across the parking lot I could see a woman standing behind the Saturn. When she saw me, she put her fists on her hips and said, "Didn't you hear your licence plate being paged?" She was short and plump. Mid-fifties.

"I beg your pardon?" I said. The bags of Ant & Grub were heavy, and I wanted to put them in the trunk of the car, but the woman was blocking my way.

"I had your licence plate paged over the P.A. system in the store. Didn't you hear it?"

I looked at her. "Why would you do that?"

"How could you *not* have heard it?"

"I asked you why you did that? Had me paged."

She pointed at the rear side window nearest her. "Is that your dog?"

"Of course it is. Who else's dog would be in my car?"

She checked her wristwatch. "She's been in there, in hundred-degree heat with the windows shut, for at least an hour!"

"*He* hasn't been in there anywhere *close* to an hour. Twenty minutes at most."

"You must have heard the page. You just ignored it."

I dropped the bags to the ground. There was a loud noise and an explosion of white dust. "For your information, madam," I said, "I'm quite fond of this dog. I walk him, I brush him, I feed him, I make sure he's got plenty of water, I pick up after him. And I did *not* hear my licence plate being paged!" My voice had risen; its pitch was thicker than normal. "Furthermore, if you'd looked carefully, you'd have seen that my window and one of the back windows are open about three inches —"

"Then why's he panting like that?"

"Because he's a dog, and it's hot, and dogs pant when it's hot. Their sweat glands are in their tongues, in case you didn't know."

She pointed again. "Why's he got his head down? *Heat prostration*, that's why!"

I could feel a black curtain falling over my eyes. I could feel myself starting to tremble. "He always has his head down like that," I said, as calmly as possible. "It's what dogs do when they're resting, which is what they do most of the time." Before I realized what I was doing, I took a step towards her. Her eyes widened and she took a step back. "Is this how you spend your Saturdays?" I persisted. "Constantly on the look out for cruelty to animals? Are you some kind of animal rights vigilante? Do you find cruelty where, in fact, none exists?" She took another step back. "That's right, keep going," I said, "get out of here."

I took another step towards her, and she began to retreat in earnest, still facing me. The side mirror of a parked car caught her shoulder and she staggered, almost falling to the pavement. "Go on," I said, "get the fuck out of here." I shooed her with my hands, as if she were a puppy in a flowerbed. "Go on, fuck off," I said, "before I go apeshit on you. Meddler. Bitch."

When I got home I was still shaking. Barbara was off in the company car showing someone a house. I put Benny in the backyard and got him a dish of water. Then I opened the trunk of the Saturn to unload the bags of Ant & Grub, but they weren't there. I'd left them where I'd dropped them in the parking lot. I couldn't face going back for them, so I started drinking instead.

When Barbara got home, I was in the living room. She looked rattled. She was impeccably dressed, as she always was, in one of her business suits, but she was flushed with the heat, and probably her excursion to the 'burbs had been a waste of time. I was sitting on her new flower-print sofa when she came in. It was hot in the house, and all I was wearing were my underpants and socks. I had everything I needed on the coffee table in front of me: a quart of Bushmills, my favourite drinking glass, a bucket of ice, an ashtray, a package of cigarettes, a book of matches, and a half-gone joint.

Barbara put her hands on her hips — in much the same way the woman at White Rose did; in much the same way Judy did this morning — and said, "How many times have I asked you not to smoke in the house?"

I tried to sit up straight. I ran my fingers through my hair.

"You're sweating like a pig on my new sofa."

I wanted to tell her about the incident at White Rose, about the woman accusing me of neglecting Benny, and how I'd reacted. I wanted to tell her about the two bags of Ant & Grub. But I didn't say anything. I just smiled stupidly. After a few moments, she shook her head and left the room.

A short time later, Reed phoned from *Sport of Kings*. "Where are you?"

"Home, obviously."

"What are you doing there? It's four-thirty in the afternoon! You didn't show up for your interview with the President of the Jockey Club. He just called. He's pissed."

"Not as pissed as I am," I said, "but it's a different kind of pissed."

It took him a while — several months — to get up the guts to fire me, and the day he did — the day I stayed home to look for the Mingus CD — Barbara fired me, too. I heard the cabby honk his horn. All she took was two suitcases and Benny. She told me not to be home the next afternoon, and she would come back for the rest of her things. I stood at the door in my underpants, drink in hand, and watched her go.

When I get back to the bar from the men's room, not only is my stool empty, but so is the one to my left. "Where'd Gordon get to?" I ask Dexter. The shot I bought him stands untouched on a Carlsberg coaster.

Dexter is pointing the remote at TV #4 and flipping through the channels. Over his shoulder he says, "Left a few minutes ago."

I swivel on my stool. Zontar is on the stool to my right, Panther has moved over one, and the two of them are talking about music, about "Sexual Healing" by Marvin Gaye.

Zontar says he's going to use it in his karaoke performance later on.

It's amazing. Fifteen minutes ago it looked like Dexter was about to be murdered, but suddenly everything's back to normal. I feel like a character in an episode of *The Twilight Zone*: something terrible happened, but somehow time has stopped and been rewound till before the terrible thing happened. The twins have resumed their snooty poses at the island, Jessy is back at the cash register, and Dexter has forgotten what the oafish man with the Chia Pet hair made me say about him.

I reach over and pick up Old Gordon's shot. I paid for it, I might as well drink it. I stop everything, close my eyes, and concentrate as it burns its way down.

When I open my eyes again, Zontar is looking at me. Beyond him I see Panther doing the same thing. Appraising me. "Scary moment there," Zontar says. "You okay?"

I nod, but can't think of anything to say.

Panther leans in front of Zontar and says, "That guy looked like he meant business. If Dexter's smart he'll take precautions."

Zontar says, "You mean like stash a gun under the bar?"

Panther says, "I was thinking more along the lines of phoning the police and filling them in on what went down."

I see Dale walking towards me.

"If Muhammad won't come to the mountain," he says, "then I guess the mountain will just have to come to Muhammad." He deposits a wad of bills on the bar in front of me.

"What's this?" I say. I look at him blankly. Then I catch on. "The fifth's already gone?"

Dale says, "Yes, the fifth's already gone." He raises his eyes to TV #1.

The prices are up. The winner, number six, paid $7, $3.30, and $3.10. I know I bet across the board, but I can't remember who I bet. I check the *Form*. "Oh," I say, "The Lorelei. That was me."

"Yes, that was you," Dale says. "Twenty across grosses you one hundred and thirty-four dollars." He pats the wad of bills on the bar. "It's all there."

I quickly peel off a fin and give it to him. I ask him how much she won by, and he says a length going away. He says he can't believe I missed the race. "I've never known you to miss a race you had money on," he says.

"I know," I tell him, "it's not like me at all, but didn't you see what happened here?"

"Didn't look that serious to me," Dale says, looking away. "Couple of boys think they're tough. Stuff like that happens, I just mind my own business. *No es muy problema.*"

A few minutes later I sense the door swinging open behind me. "It's like Grand Central in here," I say to no one in particular. I swivel around to see who it is, and it's Detective Lynn Wheeler, my old friend Campbell Young's last partner before he hung up his holster. Her current partner, Tony Barkas, stands behind her with a toothpick between his teeth. They're both in civvies: he's wearing a black leather jacket, and she's wearing a yellow ski jacket and a plaid tam.

Wheeler scans the bar, sees me, and heads my way. "Afternoon, Mr. Harvey."

"Detective."

"What's new with you?"

"Nothing much. Couple of uniforms in here not long ago looking for evidence of bookmaking, if you can imagine such a thing."

She nods. "I'm here on different business." She opens a manila folder on the bar in front of me. "You wouldn't happen to know these two characters, would you?"

I look at the photos. "I don't *know* them, but I certainly recognize them. They were in here shortly after the uniforms."

She points to the photo of the oafish man. "This one's Frank Dolan, but he goes by Mr. Clean," she says, "and the other one's known as Short Eyes, real name William Michael Geary. Short Eyes has priors for sexual interference with a minor and break-and-enter and he's done time, and Mr. Clean served eight years for manslaughter."

"Who'd he slaughter?"

"He killed his next-door neighbour with a garden spade. Released last April, and now he's wanted in Moncton, New Brunswick, concerning the death of an uncle of his whose body was found in a well."

"You should talk to Dexter," I tell her. "They threatened him."

"Threatened him?"

I spot Dexter at the cash register and wave him over. "Dexter," I say, "tell Detective Wheeler what happened."

Dexter makes a face at me. "It was nothing," he says to her.

"Mr. Harvey says they threatened you."

He shakes his head. "Mr. Harvey's exaggerating. He's just looking out for my welfare is all. It was nothing."

She points at the photos on the bar. "Is that them?"

"Yeah, that's them."

"Ever seen them before?"

"Nope, never."

"The guy with the orange hair wanted to kill you," I say.

Again, he gives me the evil eye. "All smoke, man."

Wheeler says, "You sure you've never seen him before? The guy with the orange hair."

Dexter takes a closer look at the photo of Mr. Clean. "Nah, never seen him before, not till today."

"Maybe you shouldn't be here in case they come back."

"I can handle myself. Besides, we're short-staffed."

"Dexter," I say, "he did time for murder."

He looks at me. "I told you. I can handle myself."

Wheeler says, "Detective Barkas and I are going to check out a few more places." She closes the folder and hands it to Barkas, then takes a card out of a pocket of her ski jacket and lays it on the bar. "Here's my cell. If they come back, call me. We'll swing back around in a couple of hours." Then, out of the blue she says, "So whose shift is it, anyway — Ringo or Consensus or Dale?" She surveys the tavern, but Dale's nowhere in sight. She turns back to Dexter and me. "It's Wednesday, so it must be Dale, right?" When Dexter and I shrug, she smiles. "See you in a while," she says.

SIXTH RACE

Post Time: 3:25 p.m.

(5 1/2 Furlongs.
2-Year-Olds.
Maiden Special Weight.
Purse $44,000.)

1 Motel Guest
2 Double Talk
3 Energized
4 Lazy Fly Ball
5 Prince Among Men
6 Chill in the Air
7 Fierce
8 Blue Apalachee
9 Cardinal

I make my way to the pay phone next to the entrance to the lobby and drop a quarter in the slot. I could have used the phone behind the cash register, but I want privacy. I dial Campbell Young's number.

He picks up right away. "What?" he says. I can hear a television blaring in the background.

"It's me, Priam. Am I interrupting —"

"Yeah, as a matter of fact you are. I'm in the middle of

watching two Paul Newman movies."

"*Two* Paul Newman movies?"

"*Cool Hand Luke*'s on 15, and *Hombre*'s on 18. I was just flipping around and found *Cool Hand Luke*, then it went to commercial, so I flipped around some more, and landed on *Hombre*."

"Funny, Paul Newman's name just came up a little while ago."

"You at McCully's?"

"Yes. Zontar was playing the trivia game —"

"Zontar. He's the tubby one with the suspenders, kind of geeky, wants to be a brother?"

"That's right, and there was a question about Paul Newman —"

"What was the question?"

"Well, let me see if I can remember how it was worded. It was something like 'In which movie did Paul Newman play a working-class guy named Sully Sullivan —'"

"*Nobody's Fool.*"

"That's right!"

"That's the one where Jessica Tandy plays his landlady."

"Right again."

"And Pruitt Taylor Vince plays the retard."

"I'll have to take your word —"

"And what's-her-name shows her tits."

"Melanie Griffith."

"Right. Don't try to fool me on Paul Newman."

I've known Young for twenty-five years. I knew him when he walked a beat, I knew him when he was undercover working fraud and larceny, and I knew him when he was

Homicide. I see him in here a lot. When he's not here as an investigative consultant — his term for private eye — he's here as a patron, which is most of the time. But he's a serious horseplayer, too, and back when I had my column, he always read it and always let me know what he thought of it. He didn't always like what I wrote, but the fact that he read every word was praise enough. A few years ago he asked me to use my connections to get his daughter a job at the track. Debi's a big strong girl — how could she help but be a big strong girl when her dad's six foot eight and three hundred pounds — and at the time I'm talking about she had a half-black baby and a bad attitude, but Young said she needed a chance, she absolutely loved horses, and because he had always been square with me I phoned an old acquaintance of mine, Shorty Rogers — as it turned out, Shorty was an old acquaintance of Young's, too, a former drinking buddy — out at Caledonia Downs, and he said sure, she could walk hots and muck out. That was a while back, maybe twelve years, and Debi worked for Shorty until he was murdered in 1996. I knew more than was good for me about horse racing, and because the murder was racing-related, Young, who was assigned to the case — or, more correctly, made sure it was assigned to him — asked me to help with the investigation. Which I did. The case was solved, Debi took over Shorty's barn and made a success of it, and the police department gave me a framed certificate. It's on the Wall of Fame here at McCully's — alongside autographed photos of Joe Torre, Dan Ackroyd, Bobby Orr, et cetera, as well as Ringo the Book's not-bad watercolours of Northern Dancer, Sunny's Halo, and Play the King.

But the most important connection Young and I have concerns another murder, and here I'm only going back three years to the time I asked him to help me find the man who killed my son. But that's another story.

"So listen, Campbell," I say, "I need to talk to you about a little problem down here at the bar —"

"Both *Hombre* and *Cool Hand Luke* were made in 1967, and Paul plays a kind of reluctant hero in both of them. It's kind of interesting."

"— which concerns Dexter."

"And both of them are just coming up to their climax: Luke and Dragline, the George Kennedy character, are about to get nabbed by the chain gang bosses, and in the other movie, John Russell, which is the character Paul plays, is about to get shot by the Mexican. Or maybe it's Cicero Grimes, the Richard Boone character, that shoots him, I can't remember. I'm flipping back and forth so I don't miss anything. What about Dexter?"

"Wheeler and Barkas just stopped in. They're looking for a couple of hoodlums who were here a while ago — William Michael Geary, alias Short Eyes, and Frank Dolan, alias Mr. Clean —"

"Never heard of them. What've they got to do with Dexter?"

"Dexter eighty-sixed Short Eyes earlier this after-noon, but then he came back with Mr. Clean, who, as it happens —"

"Are they there now?"

"No, but they'll be back."

"How do you know they'll be back?"

"They said so."

"So tell Dexter to go home early."

"I tried. He won't. I think he *wants* them to come back.

I think he's spoiling for a fight."

Suddenly, the sound of gunfire erupts through the phone, and Young says, "This is the part where John Russell meets his maker. Listen, if these guys show up again, give me a shout. Meanwhile, tell Dexter my advice is go home."

"I was hoping you might come down —"

"I'm retired, remember? I'm not supposed to get mixed up in this kind of thing. I'm supposed stay home and watch TV. Besides, I'm sick."

"You're sick? What's wrong?"

"Oh, me and Trick went out for dinner last night and it was his turn to choose, so we went to this Japanese restaurant — what they call a sushi restaurant —"

"I'm familiar with sushi."

"— and I didn't like the food much, but I ate it anyway — I'm not afraid to try new things — but bottom line is three o'clock this morning I'm puking up some kind of blue seaweed."

"Blue?"

"Yeah, kind of a midnight blue. And I've been on and off the shitter ever since. In fact, I'm feeling a bit iffy right now, which means I'm going to have to hang up on you, Mr. Harvey, and it probably means I'll miss the end of my goddamn movies, too."

Back at the bar, I do my calculations. I'm four for four — I laid off the one race I would have lost — and one hundred and ninety of Dale's dollars — not counting Anna's fifty — are nestled in my pants pocket. I look up and Jessy's standing there looking at me, one hand idly wiping the surface of the bar with a J Cloth.

"Hey," I say.

At her temples, perspiration has turned strands of her hair as dark as blood. Her green eyes are worried. "You okay, Mr. Harvey?"

I look back down to where I've made my calculations on the margin of the *Form*. "I'm fine, Jessy. Not to worry." I put my hands in my lap.

"I was never so scared in my life," she says, and her voice, which normally sounds as Canadian as my own, is suddenly as Irish as County Sligo. "The whole time that man had his arms around you and Gordon, the other one was staring at me."

"The one with the scar?"

She nods. "Never took his eyes off me." Then she sort of shivers. "Smiling, he was."

Maybe he'd seen the graffiti in the cubicle, I think. I reach over and pat her hand, and I'm just starting to feel better, my stomach settled and that little bit of unpleasantness behind me, when who should walk through the door, stride towards me, prop herself on Old Gordon's stool, and cross her beautiful long legs in front of me, but Anna, and I know from the look on her face she's not happy.

"Hey baby," I say, easing my hand off Jessy's. "*Quelle surprise!*"

"You bastard," she says.

"Jessy," I say, still looking at Anna, "would you please prepare a white wine spritzer for the lady."

"I don't want a white wine spritzer," Anna says.

"Hold that spritzer," I say. "What *would* you like?"

"What I would like, just once, is for you to be where you say you're going to be when you say you're going to be there."

The way she's looking at me you'd think she was

studying an old dog, deciding whether it wouldn't be a whole lot simpler just to put it down.

"Jessy," she says, without taking her eyes off mine.

"Ma'am?"

"C.C. on ice."

Anna and I have more or less been together since last winter when I was introduced to her at the Horsemen's Benevolent and Protective Association New Year's Eve Ball. Turned out we already knew each other from years before when I worked in Montreal for *Sport of Kings* and she was head secretary at Blue Bonnets Race Track. In those days I knew her just to talk to. Sometimes I had to visit her boss, Allen Prosser, the Track Secretary — the man whose job it is to decide what races to schedule: how many sprints, how many routes, how many stakes, how many claimers — to get a quotation for a column I was writing. She always nodded to me, I remember, very cool and professional. I was interested, for sure, but I was living with Sylvie at the time, not that that would have stopped me back in those days, but I knew that Anna and Mr. Prosser were often seen together, so I left well enough alone. When the meet ended we went our separate ways, and by the time I came back to Montreal the following year, she'd moved on. So it wasn't until last New Year's that we bumped into each other again. The twenty years had aged her, definitely, but in a good way. Like fine wine. She looked like a long, tall Bonnie Raitt, weathered and sexy. We filled in the blanks and, among other things, confessed that we'd each had a crush on the other back when we were slaving away at Blue Bonnets. We also discovered that we were both currently unattached. When I asked her what she was doing these days, she told me that she had married well and divorced even better. When she asked what I was doing, I was honest: I told her I'd been fired by *Sport of Kings* and was currently unemployed. She asked me what I was doing to keep busy, and I smiled my dissolute smile and made a joke about drinking enthusiastically at all hours of the day and night. And that was when she decided to make me her reclamation project, as she put it. And that's how we came to be together.

"Was I supposed to meet you somewhere?"

"Yes, you were supposed to meet me somewhere. The art gallery?"

I smack my forehead with the palm of my hand. "The Jackson Pollocks."

"That's right, the Jackson Pollocks." Then she looks at what I'm wearing and narrows her eyes. "But you're all dressed up in your plantation suit. And your Panama hat. Are you sure you forgot?"

"I always wear my plantation suit and my Panama hat, you know that."

Jessy brings the whiskey, and as Anna's knocking it back, I sneak a glance at the Blue Light clock behind the bar. Ten after three. "Well, let's go right now," I say, getting down off my stool. "We've still got time."

"No, we don't," Anna says. "It closes at four. We'd just get there and start to look around and then we'd have to leave. I won't be rushed when I'm looking at art."

"I'm so sorry, baby, I really am. How about tomorrow? We'll go tomorrow."

"We were supposed to go today."

"I know, but it completely slipped my mind. Come on," I say, squeezing her wrist, "please don't be angry. Have another drink. Stay awhile."

She doesn't say anything.

"I'm on a streak. I'm up almost a hundred dollars!"

She points her chin at me. "I'll have another C.C."

I get back up on my stool. "Dexter," I call automatically, "another C.C. for the lady!" but Dexter doesn't answer, and when I turn to look it's still Jessy behind the bar, and apparently she hasn't heard me.

"Jessy!" I call, but she's down at the far end near the cash register with her back to me, and she doesn't turn around, so I get down off my stool again and walk the length of the bar to where she's wiping ashtrays.

"Jessy," I say, "could we please get some service?"

Then she looks at me, her jungle of red hair half-hiding her flashing green eyes. "Bitch want a spritzer now, or she still drinking whiskey?"

There's some history here.

One night late last winter, about a month after Anna and I started up, I was here at McCully's, nothing unusual, betting the jugheads at Mohawk and the flats at Santa Anita or Hollywood — I can't remember now — and I had some pretty good luck. I relieved Ringo of close to five hundred dollars. So I stayed later than usual to celebrate. I recall buying a round of Duck Farts: equal parts Kahlua, Bailey's, and Crown Royal. I remember Dexter didn't have any Crown Royal, so he used Wiser's Deluxe as a substitute. Everybody loved them, so I bought several more rounds. And then things went kind of blurry until sometime near midnight when Jessy asked me if I would stay till closing time and walk her home.

In the six months that I had been a regular at McCully's, Jessy and I had formed the kind of friendship that barmaids and barflies often form, wherein, for example, the barfly, half in the bag, might make an insincere proposal of marriage, and the barmaid, pretending to be insulted, not only refuses the proposal, but insults the proposer by saying something like, "I wouldn't marry you even if you were rich, which, judging by the size of your tips, *you obviously ain't!*"

That sort of thing. All in good fun, of course, with the man laughing at the put downs and the woman smiling slightly and lowering her eyes seductively.

Well, that's the type of relationship that Jessy and I had, except she was the one saying, "When are you going to marry me, Mr. Harvey, or is it all just talk?" and I was the one saying, "Let me get back to you on that." Just the same, I was surprised that night last winter when she leaned across the bar and dragged me back from some Duck Fart–fueled reverie by saying, "Mr. Harvey, would you walk me home? It's only a few blocks, but a girl can't be too careful after closing time."

After last call, the place slowly emptied, but I stayed where I was at the bar, nursing a ginger ale until Jessy had swept the floor and tidied up the booths, and Dexter had run all the dirty glasses through their little carwash and turned off the lights over the bar and in the washrooms and the front window and the jukebox. Putting on his overcoat, he looked at me and said, "Shouldn't you be on your way?"

"Lady requested an escort," I said, nodding at Jessy, who was over by the karaoke stage, emptying the contents of her dustpan into a garbage bag.

He looked from me to Jessy and back again, then shook his head slowly.

"What?" I said. "All I'm doing is walking her home."

He raised his eyebrows. "I walked her home, too, one time," he said.

"Meaning what?"

"Girl chew you up and spit you out."

"Dexter, this is Jessy we're talking about. She's like a daughter to me."

Dexter nodded. "Yeah, well, she was like a sister to me till — look out now, here she comes."

Jessy walked up with her coat over her arm. "I'm ready."

"Let me help you with that," I said.

"You're such a gentleman, Mr. Harvey." She gave Dexter a look and said, "Too bad not everybody's such a gentleman."

As I helped her on with her coat, I glanced over her shoulder and saw Dexter waiting for me to look at him. Then he mouthed something to me. *Me hair fool.* I looked at him blankly. I shook my head. He did it again. This time I understood. *Be careful.*

Outside, she took my arm. "You're not too steady on your feet, Mr. Harvey."

"Too many Duck Farts," I said, "but the ginger ale helped."

We walked about four blocks under the streetlights, her chattering away about this and that. Next thing I remember is the long staircase up to her apartment. I can't recall whether she invited me in or whether I asked to come in or whether it was a given. All I know is there I was, sitting on her couch, trying to catch my breath. I still had my parka on with the hood up. I sat there for a long time watching a bookcase, a beanbag chair, and a television do a slow swirl in front of me.

When Jessy reappeared, she was wearing a Dallas Cowboys jersey. She had a tallboy of Foster's in one hand

J.D. Carpenter

and a pint of yogourt in the other. "I'm afraid I can't offer you a Creemore or a Bushmills," she said. She handed me the tallboy.

She lifted the lid off the yogourt container and removed a corncob pipe, a Ziploc bag, and a zebra-striped lighter.

As she filled the pipe she said, "You've smoked before, haven't you, Mr. Harvey?"

"I've been known to take a puff."

"Is it okay," she said, "if I don't call you Mr. Harvey tonight? Just for tonight can I call you Priam?"

"Be my guest."

"Just for tonight. This is a special occasion. Never to be repeated."

I looked at her. "Never to be repeated?"

"No. See, each man I sleep with, I only sleep with them once. With very few exceptions, that is."

"You're going to sleep with me?"

"Yes, I am. I've been thinking about it for a long time now. Of, course you may not want to."

"Oh no, that's fine, that's fine, but I'm curious, why do you only sleep only once with each man?"

"No strings that way. I like living alone, and even though I like men well enough, I get my fill of them at the bar. Except when I feel the urge, if you know what I mean."

She put the pipe to her mouth and lit it with the zebra-striped lighter. She sucked mightily and held her breath and closed her eyes. After she exhaled, she passed the pipe to me.

"Need some fire?" she asked huskily and offered me the lighter, but the pipe drew fine, and I shook my head and passed the pipe back to her.

"That was a pissant little toke!" she said. "Watch." She

sucked even harder and said breathlessly, "Your turn."

I took the pipe and pulled hard on it.

"Way in," she said, like a mother urging her baby to eat. "Waaaaaaay in."

In this fashion we passed the pipe back and forth. When it was done, she got up and put on some music.

I recognized it immediately. "Sonny Rollins," I said. "'After Hours.'"

Jessy said, "I know you like jazz, Priam, because you always answer the jazz questions for Zontar, and this is the only jazz CD I own. It's actually my brother's. He's a university student. Well, he *was* a university student. But never mind that. It's time we got you out of that coat — it must be stifling in there — and went for a little walk. Come along."

I got up, shed my parka, and followed her down the hall to her bedroom. There was a lit candle on each of the bedside tables. She stood in front of me and pulled the football sweater over her head. She was wearing a black bra and panties. Her breasts were large, and when she reached behind her back and unclasped her bra I watched them spill out. I looked back up at her eyes and saw gold candlelight flicker against an emerald background. She came close to me — I'd forgotten how tall she was — and I put my face into her hair, which smelled vaguely of shampoo and powerfully of cigarettes and marijuana.

She put her hands on my shoulders and pushed me gently backwards until the edge of the bed caught the backs of my knees and down I went. I'd never been on a waterbed before, and at first I felt as though I'd fallen into a swimming pool. But I wasn't alarmed. I lay there like a baby — totally trusting. Then Jessy straddled me, unbuttoned my shirt, spread it open, and slowly dragged her bare breasts up and down my chest. Her nipples were like electrodes against my skin, leaving tiny trails of shock. She leaned forward and let me suck them.

Then she rolled over on her back. I watched her breasts spread, the flesh trembling, the nipples floating solidly on their broad areolae. I touched one of them with a fingertip. The nipple and areola tilted, like a raft will when a swimmer puts his weight on the ladder, but then recovered and settled, while the surrounding flesh shivered outwards in concentric circles.

Beautiful.

And that's the last thing I remember until I became aware of Jessy prodding me in the ribs and telling me it was time to go home.

"What time is it?" I mumbled.

"Almost five."

I got dressed and stumbled down the hall to the living room. I stood there awkwardly, near the door.

"I may have to break my rule," Jessy said quietly, standing in front of me in an open dressing gown and zipping up my parka for me, "and bring you back for a second visit sometime."

I allowed myself a small smile.

"But I shouldn't have given you that toke," she added.

"Why not?" I asked. "I liked it."

I must have spoken too loudly, because she put her finger to her lips and said, "Shhh, you'll wake the Ukrainians," and pointed to the floor.

"Sorry," I whispered. "Why shouldn't you have given me the toke?"

"Because you fell asleep," she whispered back. "We never even did it!"

Walking home through the cold, empty streets, I laughed and swung my arms. At one time a failure like that would have bothered me for days, but not anymore. Now I just find things like that amusing.

All that happened late last winter, but despite what she said about breaking her rule, she hasn't invited me back. I keep dropping hints, but they don't seem to have any effect. About three weeks ago, for example, I was sitting at the bar just like I always do, drinking beer, playing the ponies. Old Gordon was sitting next to me on that occasion, too, just like he was today, until he got scared off. The difference was that instead of staring at the bank of TVs or being terrorized by louts, we were looking straight up at Jessy as she stood on the bar struggling to staple Halloween decorations to the facade above the bar. Little orange plastic jack-o'-lanterns, each one about the size of a coaster. Her feet, in their clean white socks, were inches from my fingers, and she stretched way off into the clouds above me, grunting, her arms raised above her as she worked.

Old Gordon leaned over and whispered, "Too bad she's wearing trousers. It'd be better if she was wearing one of them miniskirts."

From her aerie, Jessy said, "Gordon, you're not so far away that I can't hear you, let alone kick you in the temple and kill you."

"Sorry," he said contritely. "No offense."

Her trousers, I noticed, were green. "I've got an idea!" I called up to her, my hand cupped at the side of my mouth.

"What?" she said, looking down at me.

"I'll be Jack and you be the beanstalk."

Beside me Old Gordon started to giggle, and I gave him a quick wink. I looked back up in time to see Jessy's stapler on its way down.

A few minutes later I was standing at the basin in the men's room, holding a half dozen ice cubes wrapped in a tea towel to my forehead.

Old Gordon stood at a urinal nearby, waiting for the piss to come. "Maybe I shouldn't tell you this, Mr. Harvey," he said to the wall in front of him, "but sometimes I think about what a night of love with Miss Jessy would be like. Do you ever have such thoughts?"

So Jessy knows about Anna, but Anna doesn't know about Jessy, and I'd like to keep it that way.

I walk back along the bar to where Anna's sitting smoking a cigarette, climb aboard my stool, and point to the sixth race in my *Form*. "Help me with this one, baby. I like two horses in here, and I just can't make up my mind. I need your wise counsel."

"Give me one good reason why I should help you," she says, and lifts her nose in the air. A minute later, however, she's leaning over my *Form* saying, "Oh hell, let's see what we've got here: maiden special weight, two-year-olds, five-and-a-half furlongs." She pulls the *Form* closer and begins to scan the past performances. "Which are the two you like?"

"Well, I'm partial to Prince Among Men, but I like Double Talk, too."

"Why them?"

"These are babies, right, but Double Talk has three races under his belt, including a third last time out, and Prince Among Men, even though he's a first time starter, breezed four furlongs in forty-eight and four last Friday. He may be the one to catch."

"Why not bet the exactor?"

"No, no exactors. You know me, I usually only bet straight."

"Well, give me a minute."

I light a cigarette and look around. Panther is over at the island talking to the twins. Actually, they're reading his *Form* and pretending to listen to what he's saying. The twins never buy their own *Form*, they always borrow other people's. That's how cheap they are, they won't spend five bucks. It's odd, really, because they're serious horseplayers, and most people who know anything about horse racing will tell you you can't play the horses without a *Form*.

Zontar taps my knee from two stools over. "Mr. Harvey?"

I turn to him and he gestures upwards with his thumb. "Please."

I look up at TV #2.

WHICH MEMBER OF THE NOTORIOUS CHICAGO "BLACK SOX" BASEBALL TEAM AGREED TO "THROW" THE 1919 WORLD SERIES, YET STILL LED HIS TEAM IN HITTING WITH A HOME RUN, SIX RBIs, AND A .375 BATTING AVERAGE?

A) HAPPY FELSCH

B) CHICK GANDIL

C) JOE JACKSON

D) SWEDE RISBERG

E) BUCK WEAVER

"C," I tell him.

Then, beside me, Anna says, "Darling."

I swivel back around to face her.

"I'm ready," she says. "I've made my selection."

We move sideways through the crowd, me leading her by the hand, and when we reach Dale he says, "Ah, the beautiful Anna. Anna, why do you hang around with a reprobate like our friend here?"

"I've no idea," she replies. "He was supposed to take me to the art gallery today, but apparently he forgot."

Dale looks at me. "He forgot, did he?"

I give Dale a sour look. "As a matter of fact, I *did* forget. Not that it's any of your business. Now, if you don't mind, we'd like to place a wager."

"But it *is* my business." He turns back to Anna. "You see, my dear, if he hadn't forgotten — as he puts it — to meet you at the art gallery, I wouldn't be out ..." he checks his notes on his clipboard and, ignoring the pleading expression in my eyes, says, "... something in the neighbourhood of two hundred and forty dollars."

Anna turns to me. She's even taller than Jessy and has this very pale complexion — she calls it "fair" — which goes red if she's angry or feeling passionate. Right now her cheeks might be described as blood red, or arterial red. "I thought you said you were up a hundred." I cast daggers at Dale and say, "Good Christ, Dale, is it that much?" but it's pointless.

"Look at me," Anna says. "You did say a hundred, didn't you?"

I keep my mouth shut. There are times when it's best to keep one's mouth shut. I take her hand to lead her back to the bar, but she snatches it away.

"You bastard. You didn't forget to meet me. You didn't *want* to meet me. You wanted to spend your afternoon here, drinking and gambling. You didn't forget at all. Why do you even bother to lie? You can't lie. Whenever you lie I see right through it."

I lower my head. "I really did forget," I say, but when

I look up again she's halfway to the door. "Anna!" I shout. "Wait!"

She stops and puts her arms akimbo.

In two seconds I'm over to her. "Listen," I say, "I really did forget. I swear it."

She raises her eyes and looks at me.

"Come on," I say, "let's get out of here." I take her arm and start for the door.

"Where are we going?"

"Somewhere else. Anywhere. The Diamond."

She stops. "The Diamond! What for, more drinks? No, no, you stay here. Stay here for the rest of your miserable, pathetic life. This is exactly where you belong — here with all the other losers!"

I can feel the silence behind me, the silence from the bar and the booths and the pool table. I glance around, and it's like a tableau — everyone standing as still as mannequins, staring at us.

I drop her arm.

Then she's out the door. I want to shout to her again. But it's not, "Anna, wait!" that I want to shout. It's not, "Baby, come back, I can't live without you!" No, to be perfectly honest — and bear in mind that she's a smart woman and knows how to read a *Form* — what I really want to know is which horse she likes.

In the end I put ten across on Double Talk. By the top of the lane, however, Prince Among Men is so far in front and Double Talk is so far behind that I turn away from the television.

Behind me I can hear Panther yelling, "Prince Among Men! Prince Among Men! Come on, Prince Among Men!"

and then, "Yes! Yes! Yes! We win! We win! How about that, Ronny! How about that, Harry! We win! Handsome odds, too, by God! Nine to two! Nine to freaking two! We nailed that sucker!"

Fine. Good for you. I'm happy you and your friends have tasted success. But do me a favour. Stop trumpeting. True gamblers never trumpet. There are rules of decorum, rules of politesse, and winners never celebrate in front of losers. It's bad form, and it only leads to bad feelings, especially when one of the losers — namely me — had been very close to backing the winner himself. People don't like loudmouths, and we all know how much you want to be liked, Panther, we all know how much you want to fit in and be one of the boys, one of the regulars, one of those people who've seen the tragic underbelly of life and have lived to talk about it — one of us, in other words. So if you want to be in the club, Panther, if you really want to be in the club, show some class and shut the fuck up.

SEVENTH RACE

Post Time: 3:54 p.m.

(7 Furlongs.
2-Year-Olds, Non-Winners of Two.
Claiming $32,000.
Purse $41,000.)

1 New Country
2 Airborn
3 Delaware
4 Solo Order
5 Seize the Day
6 Papatolmenottogo
7 Foggiest Idea
8 Mind's Eye
9 Champagne Prince
10 Three Putt

I'm thinking that I may still be up a hundred and sixty, but I lost thirty dollars on that race and my sweet little streak's officially over when I become aware of a presence beside me on Old Gordon's stool and Panther's voice saying, "Nailed that sucker, Mr. Harvey! Twenty across! The twins and I — well, it was really Ronny — picked up on the jockey change. Noticed the trainer'd gone to a bugboy, and Prince Among

Men was carrying five pounds less than anybody else."

I turn to my left and face him. "Panther —"

"Ronny also pointed out that Prince Among Men's sire is Marquetry, a speed sire, and since we were only going five and a half, it all made —"

"Panther!"

He stops. "What?"

I look him steadily in the eye. "Go away. Leave me alone."

He gets that hurt look, fusses for a few seconds, then swivels around, gets off Old Gordon's stool, and goes away.

I rub my hands over my face, climb down off my stool, walk to the door, and step outside for some air. The sky's gunmetal grey, and the clouds are roiling like something out of one of those religious paintings Anna forced me to go see a few weeks ago. And even worse, it's starting to get dark. It's getting dark very early these days, which depresses me. Dark and cold. I turn up the collar of my overcoat and hold it tight at my neck with one hand while I hold my cigarette with the other. Across the street, the grandstand of the old racetrack looms. It's empty and abandoned now, nothing left but the shell. Over the years I must have climbed the stairs to the press box a couple of thousand times, but I never minded. I loved being up there — the big windows open to the breeze, the perfect panorama: below us, the punters on the apron studying their *Form*s; beyond them, the homestretch; the infield with its lake and gardens and tote board and geese; the backstretch; the barns beyond; the blue expanse of Lake Ontario serving as background to it all. Inside the press box, a men's club: racing officials, journalists, teletype operators, various hangers-on — owners, trainers, valets, retired jockeys, other characters of uncertain purpose — cigar-chomping or chain-smoking, talking and laughing and going about the business of the day in an atmosphere of sustained excitement.

I especially loved the spring meet, in March and April, when all the horsemen came back from wherever they'd spent the winter — some from Florida and Arkansas and Oklahoma, some from farms only thirty miles away, their horses' flanks still thick with winter fur. I'd walk over to the backstretch and watch the morning workouts, hoping to get a story. It wouldn't be fully light yet, and I'd stand there with the other men at the rail, smoking and stamping our feet and blowing into our coffee. The public trainers who'd been in the States would be tanned and chatty, going on about the horses they'd picked up at Tropical Park or Hialeah. The contract trainers would brag about their two-year-olds, which ones looked good, their bloodlines, their jump in the paddock. Then we'd adjourn to the track kitchen and eat breakfast and drink more coffee and smoke another three or four cigarettes.

A gust of cold air swirls around me and I tighten my grip on my collar. Of all the months, November's the worst. I'm outside as little as possible. My route from the Everdon Arms to whichever watering hole I've decided to grace with my presence is as direct as I can make it. I try to keep my eyes downcast, because if I pass a bare tree, its leaves scattered around the base of its trunk, I get depressed. In my imagination I'll turn it into a naked woman, her thin arms upraised, her colourful clothing — red and yellow and orange — in a heap at her feet, something unspeakable about to happen.

Everything dies in November, or it's already dead. And then you have to wait out four or five months of icy sidewalks and dirty snow. Like I say, I get depressed. I lost my job in November. Barbara left me in November. Such a shame, she said. Such a waste.

She called the other night — something she occasionally does — and actually caught me at home.

"Priam?"

"Speaking."

"It's me."

"Yes," I said, "I still recognize those dulcet tones." It was eightish. I had to enunciate. "To what do I owe this unexpected pleasure?"

"What are you doing?"

I was watching *Busted on the Job*, a show I quite liked. Employees caught on videotape doing things they shouldn't. I especially enjoyed the footage of a chef blowing snot into someone's supper. And the landlord who lets himself into the apartment of one of his tenants, takes some leftovers out of the fridge — it looked like a casserole dish, lasagna maybe, it was hard to tell because the quality of the film in the surveillance camera wasn't very good — removes the lid, puts the dish down on the floor, pisses in it, replaces the lid, and puts the dish back in the fridge.

"I'm watching *Busted on the Job*."

"What is it, a movie?"

"It's a new show."

"I've never heard of it. Is it good?"

I explained the premise.

She said, "Why do you watch things like that? All they do is make you black."

"They confirm my world view."

"That's what I mean."

"And you? Still watching feel-good movies?"

"They're all I watch. I don't even watch the news anymore. There's too much horror in the world. If I watch TV at all, I look for love stories, or stories about sacrifice and heroic behaviour, that kind of thing."

I took a long sip of my drink. "None of which I exemplify."

"I didn't say that."

"So why did you phone?"

"Would you rather I hadn't?"

"No, no, it's fine."

"I just wanted to see how you were getting along. How are you getting along?"

I love the girlishness of her voice. You'd never know she's a hotshot real estate agent, with her face plastered on bus shelters and park benches. "Fine, thanks."

"Did you eat tonight?"

I scratched my head. I couldn't remember. I looked towards the kitchenette, but no evidence of my having fed myself presented itself. "I'll eat later. I'm not very hungry."

Her tone, which had been friendly-curious, turned wary. "How much have you had to drink today?"

"The usual amount, I suppose. A twenty-sixer of elixir." I laughed.

"Oh, Priam."

A few moments of silence followed, a pregnant pause during which the writer of our play might be tempted to insert declarations of rekindled love, but even Barbara — whose name I never speak aloud; to do so would sully it, soil and sully it; I *think* it, however, I can't help thinking it — a self-confessed "positive vibes" junkie if there ever was one, restrained herself. Neither of us, for a few moments, said anything. What was there to say?

At length she said, "I think I'll hang up now."

"All right."

"Promise me one thing."

"What?"

"Promise you'll take better care of yourself."

"Better than what? Better than *you* took of me?"

"That's not fair —"

"Good night," I said — coolly, I hoped — and hung up. I headed for the kitchen counter where my last few ounces of Bushmills were waiting like terrified children for the ogre to seize them in his enormous fist and swallow them down.

I loosen my grip on the collar of my overcoat. I toss my cigarette butt into the street. A car zips past, but not so fast that I don't recognize the black Acura driven by the brown kid with the white turban that zipped past me when I was outside earlier this afternoon. He's on the phone, and he's obviously in a hurry — places to go, people to meet.

When I was a kid in Corning, New York, I could drop my bike on the sidewalk in front of the convenience store, and when I came back out with my Turkish Delight and my fresh pack of baseball cards, it would still be there — like Lassie. I knew all the streets of my neighbourhood and all the back alleys. I could fence-hop to all my friends' houses. We had great games of street tag and ball hockey, and one winter my pal John Lawrence George Henry Benson Carter, Junior — better known as Johnny Carter — and I collected about a hundred and forty Christmas trees people had left at their curbs for the garbagemen to pick up, and dragged them to his house and into the backyard, where we made this amazing network of tunnels and rooms that you had to crawl through. I remember the rich pine smell and the crushed snow underneath us and the womb-like chambers. We could hardly wait for the school day to end so that we could play in our maze, which we did religiously until, eventually, it lost its charm and we turned to other forms of amusement. It wasn't until late April or early May that Johnny's father made us get rid of all the trees. The snow was long gone by then, and the garbagemen must have been more than a little surprised to find a hundred and forty brown and brittle Christmas trees piled up on the lawn in front of Johnny's house.

Life was simple and sweet when I was growing up. Or so it seems to me now. My mother always wore dresses, even to vacuum. My father carved the Sunday roast. The three of us ate as a family. We had a cat named Mittens who ate at the same time we did — her bowl of food and dish of milk on the floor near the cellar door. My father hadn't started drinking yet. Mittens hadn't vanished yet.

I graduated high school and ran away to Canada. It was 1967, and there was no way I was going to Vietnam. I ended up in a YMCA in Toronto. My first jobs were at Dundas Park. I painted fences and whitewashed the cinder-block walls of the barns. I cleaned stalls and walked hots. My second summer I worked as a groom for a trainer named Clayton Armstrong. When the horses moved to Caledonia Downs for the long summer meet, he took me with him. I worked for him full-time for the next two years. Sometimes we trailered a couple of his cheaper horses out to the B-track at Fort Erie, hoping to pick up a small purse or maybe sell some old spavined gelding who couldn't cut it any longer at Caledonia. One summer we lived for three weeks in a rented house in Fort Erie. In the evenings Clayton would find himself a bar, while I was left to find my own entertainment. I would wander through the fairgrounds at Crystal Beach — past the barkers, the fun house, the Ferris wheel, the roller coaster, the smell of cotton candy, the girls walking arm in arm.

I remember those days so clearly I can picture them. It's the next quarter of a century that's a blur. I left Clayton and went to work for the *Daily Racing Form*, met Sylvie, lived with her for a while, and lost her. I bounced around the B-tracks for a few years, moved on to *Sport of Kings*, changed my surname from Wilkins to Harvey to avoid arrest as a draft dodger while I was working in the States — I chose Harvey because of Johnny Griffin's great jazz tune, "Blues for Harvey" — and stayed with *Sport of Kings* for three drunken decades, during which my stock rose and I didn't have to travel so much. I began to hobnob with the rich and famous; the rich and famous offered me money to write articles that showed them in a favourable light, and I accommodated them. In 1977, Jimmy Carter granted me amnesty: I breathed a huge sigh of relief and kept my new name. Eventually, I met Barbara and did my best to settle down, but while Barbara's career as a real estate agent accelerated, my taste for Irish whiskey accelerated, too, and my interest in writing declined.

The world changed. Toronto changed. Homeless people began to pop up like weeds, sleeping in doorways or sitting on sidewalks holding their hats out. In Corning, my father died of liver disease, and my mother, who had lived all of her life in upstate New York — in her heyday, she had been a professor of mythologies at a liberal arts college — decided she wanted to live close to me, and immigrated. I was with Barbara at the time and — on the surface, at least — respectable. My mother bought a condo in a good part of the city, but a year later her mind started to go, and I had to put her in a home. I visited regularly until she didn't know who I was anymore, and then I stopped visiting. One morning I received a phone call telling me she had been taken by ambulance to a hospital, that she was dying. When I got there, she was asleep on her back with her mouth open. I sat with her all afternoon and evening. At one point she sat up and opened her eyes. "I can't see anything," she said, and lay back down. Shortly before midnight I listened to her body empty itself of air.

My taste for Irish whiskey became a hunger that spiraled out of control. Insatiable, I was. The ten thousand dollars my mother left me — she donated the rest of her money to the classics department of the college where she had taught — I exhausted in six months of drinking and gambling. Barbara left me and I lost my job, I moved back to the old Dundas Park neighbourhood and took a furnished apartment at the Everdon Arms. I became a barfly, and every race day I walked across the street from McCully's to the track and played the ponies. Then the track closed. Now it's just a derelict old grandstand the fat cats are tearing down to make way for a housing development that's going to make them even fatter. And speaking of McCully's, what with the races on TV, bookies on the premises, an ATM machine beside the door to the lobby, drinks at the bar, food in the kitchen, and Dexter and Jessy to look after me, I no longer have any need to go outside. If I was really smart I'd accept the inevitable and move upstairs into the Hearth&Home

with all the other reprobates. Then I wouldn't have to go outside at all.

I go back inside.

Panther — his feathers still ruffled, no doubt — is standing at the island with the twins. I climb back on my stool and stare ahead at nothing. Gradually, I become aware of the bottles of liquor displayed in front of me. Triple Sec, Bailey's, O'Darby. Tia Maria, Kahlua, Drambuie. Stock Vermouth, Smirnoff Vodka, Bacardi Rum. Sauza Tequila, Wild Turkey, Jack Daniel's. Canadian Club, Wiser's Deluxe, Johnny Walker Red. To the right of the bottles is a mirror. In it I can see a partial reflection of the big-screen TV across the room. There's a football game on. Jets versus the Bills. Except today's Wednesday, and there's no game on Wednesday. It must be highlights from last weekend. In the mirror I watch slow motion footage of a quarterback dancing in the pocket before delivering a pass.

"Dexter," I say, "a Bushmills, please."

What else? Anna's gone. Again. I stand her up again, she walks out again. But she'll be back. Woman still thinks she can save me. Sooner or later she'll get the picture.

And once again I've told Panther to leave me alone, and once again he's slunk off wounded. But he'll be back, too.

Why is that? Why do they keep coming back? Why won't they leave me alone?

Last Friday night, for example. I had convinced Anna that The Rex Hotel was the place to be — or in her case, to be seen. The Rex is a jazz bar, and when we got there, around ten, the band had already been playing awhile, it was standing room only, and we ended up stuck behind a pillar. Halfway through the set, a few people left and we grabbed two bar stools. As Anna argued with the bartender about the quality of the wine in her spritzer, I watched a bespectacled man in a brown toque and a black turtleneck smiling beatifically at nothing and playing phantom drums at his table, beating the smoky blue air with his fists.

When Anna shouted, "What an ostentatious asshole!" into my ear, I didn't know if she was referring to the bartender, the man in the toque, or me.

The band was cooking. They played "My Favorite Things," "Moment's Notice," and "Naima," good, long versions of each. You know you're in a real jazz bar when the waiters and waitresses stop what they're doing to applaud at the end of each solo. You know you're in a real jazz bar when street people stand shoulder to shoulder with CEOs and their secretaries — all of them bobbing their heads in perfect synchronicity.

The band took a break, and a few minutes later I found myself talking to the guy on the stool next to mine. Turned out we had similar tastes — Dexter Gordon, David Murray, Roland Kirk. At one point I was telling him about the *Mingus at Carnegie Hall* album and about Roland Kirk "cuttin'" George Adams "at his own shit," when Anna poked me hard in the shoulder.

I turned my head. "What?"

"You're ignoring me."

"I'm just talking," I said. "It's not every day I meet someone I can talk jazz with."

"Jazz is boring. And furthermore, you shouldn't be talking to a stranger when I'm sitting right here beside you. It's rude."

"No, actually you're the one who's being rude."

She bit her lip. "I'm going."

"Fine," I said. "Go. I'm having a good time, this is a good bar, the music's excellent, and I'm staying." I gestured towards my untouched beer, waiting on its coaster like a good soldier. "I'm hardly even drinking, for christsakes."

Deliberately, unsteadily, she set her wineglass down on the bar. She must have had a couple or three during the previous set or while I was talking, and I hadn't noticed. "Why is it," she said, "that you never want to get drunk with me? The only times you get drunk — and we both know there are plenty of those — are when you're at McCully's, or when you're with a complete stranger, or when you're alone? Why is that?"

I waited her out, then said, "I told you, I'm not getting drunk. I didn't come here to get drunk, I came here to listen to jazz."

She slowly dismounted from her stool and adjusted the strap of her bag over the shoulder of her jacket. She stood there, swaying in front of me for thirty seconds, then she did an about-face and disappeared into the crowd.

It was an all-Coltrane night, as I soon came to realize, and in the next set the band — two tenor saxes, piano, bass, drums — moved smoothly from "Lonny's Lament" to "Harmonique" to "Giant Steps."

I finished my beer and ordered another. During the next intermission, the man beside me and I complained to each other about a new morning DJ we'd both heard on a local FM jazz station who played too many vocals, too many cuts from commercial albums that important musicians made during periods of weakness or poverty or bad judgment — *Coltrane Plays Your Christmas Favourites; Ornette Coleman: Just for Kids;* that sort of thing — and thought Clifford Brown played the saxophone — and then, about five minutes into the first tune of the fourth set, I decided to leave. I probably felt guilty, probably felt some remnant of the kind of domestic guilt I used to feel towards Barbara before I dulled it with drink. This, of course, was after I'd *caused* it with drink. Anyway, I said goodbye to my new friend and started towards the exit, likely with the idea in mind of phoning Anna and apologizing.

I made it as far as the door, which was right beside the stage. One of the tenor players, Pat LaBarbera, was in mid-solo, nodding and weaving like a fighter. Two feet away from me, the other tenor man, Kirk MacDonald, drank deeply from his pint glass and lit a cigarette, the whole time tapping his foot and moving his head to the music. I can't leave this, I thought to myself. How can I leave this? And furthermore, why should I leave this? I wove my way back through the crowd to the bar. A young woman had claimed my stool, but it didn't matter. My acquaintance was still there and I ordered another beer. When the tune ended, LaBarbera stepped up to the mike and said, "Thank you, thank you. For our next number we would like to play 'Chasin' the Trane.'" I looked at my friend and we both smiled. We settled in for fifteen minutes of bliss, that particular kind of bliss that only jazz can provide, where you become mindless and alert at the same time, and the external distractions around you — the clinking of glasses, the murmur of voices, someone elbowing past you on his way to the can — are of no consequence. The only thing that matters is the music. Two tenor saxes honking contrapuntally. The pianist punctuating with single notes. The bassist running up and down the scales like a man on a ladder. The drummer's head, bopping hard, whipping sweat into the audience. All of them working independently; all of them working together. Water rushing over stones. Different colours, different shapes.

At some point I found myself in the men's room. Fruit flies were hovering over the urinals. The man next to me was either asleep or passed out, his forehead pressed against the wall, his ball cap tipped up by its brim. He smelled powerfully of piss, or maybe it was just the general stink of the room. In one corner, the stoned man in the brown toque was no longer beatific; he was messed up, alternately grinning and frowning, babbling about his lord and saviour. Gesticulating. Stamping his foot.

I have no idea what time I got home. I never did phone Anna, but what kills me is she still won't leave me alone, still thinks she can stop my boozing and gambling, still thinks she can save me from myself. Give it up, I want to tell her, it's hopeless. You're wasting your time. You and Barbara should start a club. You could meet Tuesday nights in a church basement and call yourselves "Survivors of Priam Harvey." You could give testimonials about how frustrating it is to try to help someone who won't help himself.

Dexter has placed my Bushmills before me. I don't think I should have ordered it. I've had my fill. I stare at it like a little boy stares at a door he knows he shouldn't open. I lift it off the bar, my hand shaking so much that some of it slops over the rim, and down it. I almost forget to taste it, then I remember to, but can't seem to taste much of anything. I can feel it burn though. No problem there.

I guess Old Gordon's gone for the day. Worried about the wife. Or worried about the second coming of Mr. Clean.

At the far end of the room, Zontar's singing. *"Ooh, ooh,*

bet you wonder how I knew ... " The twins stand like statues at the island, their pints held at chest level, the expressions on their faces unchanging and identical, two men of no particular talent who, by virtue of British ancestry, hold themselves above the rest of us.

Pip pip.

Time stops for a moment. Dexter is fixed in position leaning into the freezer for a frosted beer mug, his black face illuminated from below. At the far end of the bar, Jessy is looking right at me, an expression of concern frozen on her face.

Someone's playing with my hearing. Zontar's voice has gone baritone and slow as molasses. *"Some other guy that you knew before ... "*

There's a metallic taste in my mouth. A loud buzzing in my ears. Beads of sweat pop out on my forehead and temples. I can feel them. I reach in slow motion for a napkin to wipe them away. I feel cold and clammy. I start to float up off my stool towards the ceiling. My head throbs, and the sound in my ears begins to pulsate. *"Took me by surprise, I must say ... "* I try to speak but the noise comes out my ears, and there's no meaning to it, just a dull roar, a bellow. Then everything fades, slowly, to black.

When I can see again, I'm curled up on the floor of a small cave. Wrapped in a fur blanket. Warm and calm.

Candle flame casts an orange glow on the curved walls and rounded ceiling. I watch the movement of light and shadow. They dance together, but they don't blend or mix.

I'm not frightened.

I feel rested. Happy.

I close my eyes.

* * *

I open my eyes.

An oval of faces looking down at me.

Jessy. The twins. Dale, Dexter, Panther. One or two I don't recognize. It's like a camera looking up from ground level at the faces of football players in a huddle.

"What happened?" I say. I turn my head and see a pair of dirty running shoes with grey sweat pants stretching up from them. I turn to the other side. More shoes. I close my eyes again, but the cave isn't there anymore.

Someone says, "You passed out."

Another voice says, "Toppled right over, man."

I can hear giggling.

A damp cloth is pressed against my face. It feels cool. I open my eyes.

At the end of the arm holding the cloth Jessy says, "Are you okay, Mr. Harvey?"

I'm cold, shivering, but otherwise fine. Rested. I close my eyes.

Dexter's voice says, "Ready to get up?"

I think about this for a while. I understand that an answer is expected. "Can't I just stay where I am?"

For some reason this makes people laugh. I open my eyes. The twins tower above me, laughing and shaking, their beer mugs held to their chests. "Ronny and Harry," I say up at their blurry faces, "it may interest you to know that I, too, am bred in the purple." Their faces are muzzy. I can't gauge the effect I'm having. "Edward the Second," I tell them, "and a milkmaid. Issue name of Captain Harvey, whence cometh, many generations later, yours truly — a royal bastard." Beyond the twins' heads I see the bank of televisions. Shannon Brown comes into focus; she's looking down at me from TV #3. Eight years old. She's smiling. She trusts whoever is taking her picture.

Dexter says, "Come on, Mr. Harvey, let's get you up."

He and Panther lean down close to me and suddenly up I go.

I'm standing.

I'm closer to Shannon now. Now she's sixteen, computer-enhanced.

I'm a little wobbly, a little woozy.

"How 'bout it? Can you stand up by yourself?"

"Dexter," someone says, "can we please get something else on number four? Nobody in here gives a shit about golf."

Panther's voice says, "I'll stay with him."

Someone else says, "Give him a shot of that whiskey he likes, that'll fix him up!" and there's more laughter.

Before I know it I'm back on my stool. Someone plops my hat on my head. I take a deep breath and exhale slowly. A hand appears and places a glass of water in front of me.

I clear my throat and light a cigarette. "When I was a rookie journalist," I say to Panther, who is sitting beside me, "the Irish trainer Sean McKay invited me to breakfast — this was at Blue Bonnets in Montreal — because he had a couple of stories he wanted to tell me. Sean was a former jockey, he looked like a leprechaun, and his breakfast was vodka and orange juice. The first story he told me was about falling off a horse in a steeplechase at Aintree and waking up in the hospital — him on one table, his stomach on another; a hoof had opened him up like a tin can — and the second story was about a fix he had been asked to take part in. Another trainer had come up to him the day before our breakfast and said, 'Sean, you've got a horse in the third race Thursday night, right?' and Sean said, 'Yes,' and the trainer said, 'Well, so-and-so's going to win the race, his kids need new shoes,' or something like that, 'so make sure your boy knows what to do.' Rather than take part, Sean scratched his horse — Impetuous Red was the horse's name — then invited me to breakfast and told me he wanted me to write a piece about it. He was taking quite a chance because the leak could have easily been traced back to him, but he insisted. He was an honourable man and bound and determined to do his bit to clean up horse racing. Well, I wrote the piece and submitted it to my editor in Toronto, who phoned me about an hour later to tell me he'd killed it. 'Why?' I said. 'You told me I could write about whatever I thought was newsworthy.' 'You *can* write about whatever you think is newsworthy,' he said, 'as long as *I* think it's newsworthy, too. And as long as it promotes horse racing, as long as it shows horse racing in a favourable light. A piece about a fix — whether it's true or not — does not, I'm sure you'll agree, show horse racing in a favourable light.' Anyway, to make a long story short, the race went off as planned, the betting public was cheated, a few guys in the know made themselves some money, and I settled into a long and prosperous career writing crap."

"It wasn't crap," Panther says.

"It *was* crap, it was *all* crap except for one other piece I wrote when I was working at Windsor Raceway, a month or two after the Blue Bonnets meet ended. It was about three grooms from Rhode Island who'd gotten in some kind of drug trouble and were ruled off all American tracks for life. So they crossed into Canada at Detroit, got jobs at Windsor Raceway, and I wrote about them starting over, getting back on their feet. A local trainer hired them, and their future was beginning to look bright. I sent the piece in, and not only was it killed, but the next day the FBI paid me a visit. Two big guys in dark suits came into my cubicle and grilled me about the three grooms. When they left I phoned my editor. I told him what had happened, and he said, 'I thought I made myself clear when I nixed that piece you wrote about the fix at Blue Bonnets.' 'Oh,' I said, 'I guess I'm a slow learner.' He said, 'This is a business, for fucksake. You're a reporter, not a social worker. You think a piece about crackheads in the backstretch is good for the image of horse racing?'" I lift my glass of water and drain it. "So I finally came to understand that, journalistically speaking, my hands were tied."

Panther says, "What happened to the three grooms?"

"Beats me. Never saw them again. And I didn't go looking for them, either. It was definitely my editor who put the FBI onto them, and my guess is they were escorted back across the border and returned to the same ghetto that spawned them. Anyway, I started writing what my editor wanted. Inoffensive pieces. Some rich guy wants a piece about how his wife names their horses after their grandchildren, I write it. Some agent wants me to promote his jockey and there's fifty bucks in it for me, I do it. On the other hand, if there's a spill and some horse dies on the track, or if some jockey drops his whip and a couple of Duracells fall out, or if some old gelding collapses in his stall and when the vet gets there the horse's head's still bleeding from the beating he took, I ignore it because it isn't good for the image of horse racing." I lean forward so I can see down the bar. "Dexter," I call, "a pint, please, when you get a chance."

Panther says, "Are you sure you should, Mr. Harvey, you just —"

"Fights and corruption and greed," I tell him. "I saw more fistfights than I can remember. I saw fistfights in the shedrow and the track kitchen and the press box. In the winner's circle one time, I watched a trainer named Calhoun punch another trainer in the nose just as the picture was being taken. As for fixes, when I worked the B-tracks, especially Montreal, I always knew when the fixes were in. And at the end of the night I had to walk past these welfare cases going through fistfuls of tickets they'd gathered off the floor, hoping to find something someone had dropped by mistake, something cashable. Sometimes they had their kids with them, sound asleep beside them on the bench, everybody gone home but them. I watched many people ruin themselves gambling. Literally ruin themselves. Lose their savings, destroy their families."

Dexter places my pint in front of me. "Go easy, Mr. Harvey," he says.

I nod and say, "The worst fix I ever saw involved a girl named Lureen Martin. Her dad, Woodrow Martin, had come up from Oklahoma with a string of bush-circuit thoroughbreds. Meanwhile, Lureen was a cheerleading major at a state college in Elk City, Oklahoma, if you can believe it, but what she really wanted to be was a jockey. Well, nothing was too good for Woody's little girl, so he flew her up to Windsor for her first race. Woody wasn't big or strong, but he was crafty, and he had an entourage of unpleasant relatives and a reputation for hurting people who didn't do what he wanted them to. So when he asked me to write a piece about Lureen's big debut, I was afraid not to. I was afraid I'd wake up in the middle of the night with a flashlight in my face. So I wrote the piece, and it was published the day of her first ride. There was even a photo of Lureen — dumb as a post, but cute as a button." I take a sip of my beer and wipe my mouth with a napkin. "Woody was very happy with the piece."

Panther says, "I assume she won."

I laugh. "Woody had that race so fixed the other jockeys had to stand up in their irons and haul back on their reins to keep from passing her. She was 20-1 on a piece of dog meat called Seashell that hadn't won a race in three years, and when she won, going away, nobody said boo, not even the stewards."

"Did you have money on her?"

"Everybody had money on her. Everybody in the know, that is. That horse should have been *90*-to-1. And just to give you an idea of what Woody was like, that night he invited a bunch of us out to a roadhouse called Frank's to celebrate her victory. His treat. Well, we'd just finished supper at this big round table — trainers and writers, a couple of jockeys, three or four women. Everybody was drunk. Woody's nephew Hoyt was leaning back in his chair singing 'I Walk the Line' at the top of his lungs. Woody'd paid the bill and was just putting his wallet back in his vest pocket when the bouncer asked Hoyt to quiet down, he was bothering the other patrons. Hoyt stood up and took a swing at the bouncer. The women screamed, and the bouncer — a big, crewcut, three-hundred-pound farm boy — picked Hoyt up and threw him through a plate glass window into the parking lot. Made a sound like a car crash. So Hoyt's father Verlyn went after the bouncer, and the bouncer knocked Verlyn down and stomped on his leg. That was another interesting sound. Then it was Woody's turn. He stood up — more on principle than anything, I think — and *he* took a shit-kicking. I retired from the field about that time, and when I saw Verlyn and Woody a couple of days later, Verlyn's leg was in a cast and one whole side of Woody's face was purple and yellow. Hoyt was still in hospital. But the end of the story goes like this: two weeks after the fight at Frank's Roadhouse that farm boy bouncer went missing." I pause to take a breath. "Never seen again."

"Wow," Panther says. "Where was Lureen during all this?"

"No idea. She wasn't even there for her own celebration. Maybe she was underage — she looked about fourteen — or maybe Woody had her locked up in a motel somewhere. She was a sexy little thing — looked like a young Sally Field — and I'm sure he had to use a tight leash on her. What race is it?"

Panther looks up at TV #1. "The seventh, but there's only about a minute to post."

"That's okay," I say, "I have to visit the men's room. We'll sit this one out and play the eighth."

"Actually," Panther says, sort of sheepish, "I've already made a bet. The twins ... well, Ronny, actually, recommends the six horse."

"Well, you're all set then, aren't you."

The problem with the crapper at McCully's — besides the fact that most men are such pigs that they would rather piss all over the seat than lift it — is there's nothing to read. I like to read on the crapper and I can easily spend half an hour in such fashion. Sometimes I get so engrossed I forget where I am. In my bathroom at the Everdon I have quite a library. I have a stack of old *Racing Forms* two feet high, thirty-one years worth of *Sport of Kings* magazines, a small collection of adult reading — vintage copies of *Gallery* and

Cavalier — and, best of all, I have my catalogues. I'm not talking about Sears catalogues with their photos of women in underwear, or Victoria's Secret catalogues with their photos of unbelievable women in underwear, I'm talking about my collection of horse auction catalogues. Because I was in the business, I'm still on the mailing list of the auction companies — just in case I want to write about any of the horses being offered for sale — and over the years I've collected hundreds of them, maybe thousands, several hundred of which are piled up in my bathroom. Each one is the size of a pulp novel, and each page is devoted to one horse. For instance, let's take a yearling colt, Hip #115, that was offered for sale at Saratoga last August. I've memorized his breeding through the first three dams. His father is Gone West and his mother is Dance Swiftly, by Danzig — a son of Northern Dancer. He's beautifully bred and brought a ton of money, I'm sure — maybe a million dollars, or more. His mother was unraced, but she's a full sister to Dance Smartly, the greatest race mare in Canadian thoroughbred history. Dance Smartly won twelve races and over three million dollars, was named horse of the year in Canada, champion three-year-old filly in North America, and not only won the Queen's Plate, but has herself produced two Queen's Plate winners, Scatter the Gold and a squished-name filly, Dancethruthedawn. Dance Smartly's mother, Classy 'n Smart, was champion filly at three in Canada, and was half-sister to two millionaires, Sky Classic and Regal Classic. This is a very strong family, and if I'd been at Saratoga last August with a bucket of gold between my feet, I'd have bought Hip #115.

Because I've never actually seen the colt, I like to imagine what he's like. A golden chestnut, two of his legs would have stockings, and his face would have the narrow, well defined blaze his great grandfather Northern Dancer had — running down from the forehead and swerving over the left nostril. I love the markings on horses' faces — stars, snips, blazes. And I love their body colours, too — light bay, dark bay, blood bay, mahogany bay, chestnut, liver chestnut, roan, grey, black.

		Raise a Native
	Mr. Prospector	
		Gold Digger
Gone West		
		Secretariat
	Secrettame	
		Tamerett

Hip #115
Chestnut Colt

		Northern Dancer
	Danzig	
		Pas de Nom
Dance Swiftly		
		Smarten
	Classy 'n Smart	
		No Class

I think if I were ever able to own such a horse I would die a happy man. Even if he never won a race I would still love him. I could visit him and stroke his nose and feed him carrots and sugar cubes and tell him how handsome he is, how noble. I would prefer his company to the company of any man or woman I've ever known. I would prefer his company to my own.

I step out of the cubicle, and while I'm at the basin splashing cold water on my face, a man I've never seen before comes into the men's room. He's medium height, balding, fortyish. Unremarkable, really, except for the scruffy motorcycle jacket he's wearing. I turn and watch him position himself at a urinal. The crest on his back reads:

DEVIL'S DEMONS
M. C.
"DRIFTER"
NIAGARA CHAPTER

While I'm watching him, he glances at me, then does a double take. He says, "Not very often you see somebody dressed up in a white suit."

"It's a plantation suit," I say, "and I'm not 'dressed up,' I wear it all the time."

"Oh, a plan*ta*tion suit, is it?" he says to the tiles in front of his face. "Looks more like a *fag* suit to me. Fag hat, too." He smiles and shakes his head. "I saw you fall off your stool out there. You don't own no plantation, you're a drunk is all you are. And pitiful, too."

I turn away from the basin, pump a couple of feet of paper towel from the dispenser, dry my hands and face, and toss the balled-up paper into the waste basket. I look at the man for a moment — he's still shaking his head and smiling — then push open the door of the men's room and walk back into the noise and smoke of the bar.

And into a scene of jubilation. Over at the island, Panther is pounding one of the twins on the back and making a lot of unintelligible noise.

I stop beside Dale. "What's the occasion?"

"Twins hit again," he says dourly, "with your young friend riding their coattails."

"Who won it?"

"The six."

I lean over his clipboard. "Papatolmenottogo."

"That's right."

"Another horse with a squished name. Is God abandoning us, Dale? Is he setting us adrift?"

"He seems to be. Twins are suddenly up and I'm suddenly down."

I peer through the smoke towards the island, and it's as if Ronny and Harry are waiting for me to look at them because they're both staring straight at me, smug smiles on their faces. Together they raise their pints in mock salute.

Behind them, beaming in all directions, his cheeks flushed, his arms around their shoulders as if he were the proud father of prematurely aging twins, Panther shouts, "He's the heavy hitter, our Ronald, he's the man of the hour! He's in charge! In charge of all winners! He's the oracle, the fount, the light! He's blessed, ladies and gentlemen! Kneel at his feet as he reveals the word, the word being the name, the name being the winner of the eighth race, upcoming and imminent!"

EIGHTH RACE

POST TIME: 4:23 P.M.

(1 1/4 MILES. TURF.
4-YEAR-OLDS AND UP.
STARTER ALLOWANCE.
PURSE $28,000.)

1 CLARENCE BROWN
2 STAYER
3 THREAD THE NEEDLE
4 SOLDADO [BRZ]
5 FLY IN
6 ULUVITNUNOIT
7 SPYGLASS
8 DIXIELANDER
9 ELUSIVE

That there's another horse with a squished name in the eighth race should come as no surprise. World's full of horses with squished names. It's a fact and it's a sorry fact, but it is, after all, reflective of what's going on — not only among horses, but among human beings. For centuries, people gave their kids good strong traditional names like John and William and Margaret and Elizabeth, but in the last twenty years we've got a whole new crop of names like Tyler and Brandon and Madison and Kayla — never even on the charts before, but here they are — and every grade four class in the Western world has four Ethans in it, three Austins, a couple of Chloes, and a Cassidy (or, better yet, Kassidee), and black people, my God, they're giving their kids names like Kyesha and LaTondra and Shaquille, African-*sounding* names, but they're no more African than I am, they're trend names, fashion names, they're black TV names just the way Skyler and Cody and Harmony are white TV names, they have no history to them, no lineage, no substance. It's all crap — like Wal-Marts, where they greet you like you're family, and chain restaurants where the servers drop everything and gather round your table to sing "Happy Birthday" when all you want to do is eat your quesadillas but you can't because these minimum-wage high-school dropouts with barbed-wire tattoos and infected navels are pretending they give a shit about you.

Nor should it come as any surprise that this race's squished-name horse is coming out of the six-hole, as did the squished-name winner of the last race, which makes you ask yourself what are the chances of horses with squished names winning two consecutive races from the same post position?

Answer? Entirely possible, if said horses happen to be the best in their field on this particular day. It's not the horse's fault his dumb-ass owners named him Papatolmenottogo anymore than it's the little black girl's whose parents named her Sha-Nee'qua. So here we have Uluvitnunoit, which the chalk bettors will jump all over because he won his last race, whereas I will try to keep an open mind as I study the past performances of all the horses in the race, aware at the same time of my bias towards classical names, names such as Stayer and Thread the Needle and Elusive.

"Dexter?"

"Mr. Harvey?"

"A shot of Bushmills, please."

Most of these horses are old claimers — Clarence Brown is ten years old, Soldado is eight — but as it happens, Uluvitnunoit is only four. He lacks experience, but he has the benefit of youth. And, like I say, he won his last start. On the grass, no less, which happens to be today's surface of choice. I feel a change coming on. I may have to break one of my sacred rules. I may have to bet a horse with a squished name.

I hear a voice behind me. "Why don't you just get the fuck out of here!" it says, and I look up at Dexter, standing across the bar from me, a shot glass in one hand and my bottle of Bushmills in the other, and he's looking over my shoulder.

"There's a familiar sound," I say, "but surely it can't be him."

Dexter nods. "It's him."

I swivel on my stool and look across the room, and there he is, complete with tartan scarf and fluorescent pink trucker's cap, shaking his fist in Zontar's face.

"You're like a nightmare!" he exclaims. "If you can't sing something mellow, something by Frank or Tony or Mel, then just get the fuck out of here! I can't stand that Motown shit!"

"Finn Boyle!" I shout.

He turns and peers across the bar at me. "Did I leave my cane here?" he shouts back, as if it were yesterday and not six months ago that we last crossed paths.

"Behind the bar," I tell him. "Dexter's been taking care of it for you. Come here and sit down, let me buy you a drink."

"Who's the Motown wannabe?" he says, jerking his thumb backwards. "I don't remember him."

"That's Zontar," I say. "He's okay."

Finn Boyle settles himself on Old Gordon's stool. "He's a fucking nightmare is what he is," he says, shaking his head. He looks at Dexter, who's waiting for him to name his poison. "You really take care of my cane?"

Dexter takes a few steps to his left, reaches under the bar, returns to where we're sitting, and presents the walking stick to Finn Boyle. Its shaft is sleek and black, and the knob at its top is as big and gnarled as an old man's fist. Finn Boyle accepts the walking stick, props it between his knees, and turns to me.

"You're sitting on my stool."

I'm momentarily taken aback, but only momentarily. "You told me to. Before you went away. Don't you remember?"

"Maybe I do, maybe I don't."

"You want it back, you can have it back."

Finn Boyle scowls. "Don't know how long I'll be staying. You keep it for the time being. What's that shooter you used to order?"

"You mean a Duck Fart?"

Finn Boyle looks at Dexter. "Make me a Duck Fart. A big one. In a tumbler, lots of ice. He's paying," he says, and tilts his head at me.

"So, Finn," I say, as he reaches in front of me for one of the bowls of Bits & Bites that Jessy's distributed along the bar, "rumour has it you got out of the joint last summer. Where've you been?"

His mouth full of Shreddies and pretzel pieces and those little lozenge-shaped cheese-tasting things, Finn Boyle says,

"It's a long story. I spent a few months on the pipelines in
Alaska, then took a bus down the coast to Mexico, drank a
lot of tequila in Tijuana, shacked up with a hooker named
Juanita, then, when my stash was bottoming out I contracted
onto a three-masted schooner, name of *Bountiful*, bound
for Acapulco, crewed out of there on a sloop headed for
Mazatlan, survived a hurricane in which my captain was
swept overboard, limped into port just north of San Diego,
stayed with a lady I knew there for a while, bought a very
pricey bus ticket to Buffalo, New York, took a cab from there
to my sister's in North Tonawanda, recuperated there for a
week, took another cab to the border, caught a Greyhound
to Toronto, and here I am."

Finn Boyle reaches for more Bits & Bites. I know better
than to challenge him, to say, for example, "What *really*
happened? What did you *really* do?" because I don't want
him going apeshit on me. My guess is he was holed up
the whole time in a hostel over by Moss Park, where the
rummies go to lick their wounds. That, or he was with his
sister until he could get it together to come back here. Mind
you, I don't know why anybody would want to come back
here. Maybe his sister kicked him out.

I don't know what it is about Finn Boyle, why I like him
so much. After all, he's a liar, he's violent, he's unpredictable,
one minute he's your friend, the next minute he'll stab
you just for looking sideways at him, he's completely
untrustworthy, he'll drink your beer or steal your last
smoke while you're gone for a leak. I don't know what it is.
It makes no sense to admire a man like Finn Boyle, but I do.
I think maybe it's because despite all his bad habits and his
negative qualities, he's a fighter. He won't back down from
anybody. And despite all his bad luck — the broken hip,

the broken leg, the blind eye, the wife running off — he's a survivor. I think it's self-esteem that keeps him going. He still thinks he's right — it doesn't matter about what. And even with that frog eye, Finn Boyle still thinks he's attractive to women, still hits on them fearlessly and shamelessly, and, to hear him tell it, they can't get enough of him.

I glance up at TV #1. Five minutes till post. I pat Finn Boyle on the shoulder, climb off my stool, and walk over to where Dale is recording a bet for one of the twins.

"Duly noted," I hear him say. "Five win, five show on *el numero dos.*"

"That's Stayer, right?" the twin says. "I don't speak Italian."

"*Si, bueno.*"

The twin turns and sees me, and it's Harry. I know it's him because his nose is veinier than Ronny's. He smiles vaguely, but he's not so cocky up close.

"Twenty across on the six, please," I say to Dale.

Dale begins to write down the information, then stops. "You're aware you're betting a horse with a squished name?"

"Yes, Dale, I'm fully aware. I happen to believe he'll win."

Back at the bar, I knock back the Bushmills Dexter brought me. I gesture to Jessy, and when she comes over, I say, "Has Vinnie got anything in the kitchen fit to eat?"

She takes a pencil from behind her ear, bites once, gently, on the eraser, and says, "All he's got is burgers and, let's see, I think he's still got some of those ribs like the ones Gordon had, and chicken fingers and chicken wings and fries and salad. The salad's actually fresh."

"In that case I'll have a burger and salad."

"Bacon and Swiss and fried onions on the burger?"

"No, thank you."

"Nothing? That's what you usually have."

"Today's different. Today you see before you a new man."

"And you usually have the fries, not the salad."

"This is true, but like I say, I'm a new man today. Firstly, my dear, I'm betting a horse with a squished name, and secondly, I don't want anything on my burger."

"What about the salad?"

"Nothing on the salad, either. Plain and simple for the troubled stomach. Hell, I don't even want a fork. I'll eat it with my fingers."

Beside me Finn Boyle says, "Does his burger come with fries?"

"Salad *or* fries," Jessy says. "Mr. Harvey ordered the salad."

"I just thought if he didn't want the fries, I'd eat them."

"As I said, his meal doesn't —"

"Jessy, sweetheart," I interrupt, "a side of fries as well, please." I turn to Finn Boyle. "Gravy on those fries?"

He considers. "Is it one of those powder mixtures or is it real gravy?"

Jessy puts her hands on her hips and tilts her head. "It comes in a can."

"Okay, I'll have the gravy."

Above me, on TV #1, the yellow-jacketed members of the gate crew are loading the horses.

"Dexter," I say, "a little volume on #1."

Dexter picks up a remote and points it at the television.

Spyglass and Thread the Needle break alertly, and it's quickly evident that both horses want the lead, the result being a blistering opening quarter, bad strategy considering they've still got a full mile to run. My horse is two lengths back in third, and I'm already questioning my jockey's decision to stay so close to the pace. It's another eight lengths back to the rest of the field, but that means nothing early on in a route race. They maintain their positions down the backstretch, but as they move into the far turn my jockey makes his move, catches the leaders mid-turn, and by the head of the stretch is alone in front. But moving up on the outside like a matched team are two other horses, the five and the nine, and halfway down the stretch my horse's head begins to hang, and the five and the nine blow by him. My only hope is that he can hold on for third, but then another horse's head appears at the left of the TV screen, and in the final few yards he not only thunders past my horse, but past the five and nine as well, and wins going away by at least a length and a half, the black number on his white saddlecloth a very visible two.

Behind me I can hear Panther bellowing. "Stayer stayed! Stayer stayed! He came, he saw, he stayed! Twins rule! Our man Harry is the man of the hour! First Ronny, then Harry! How can you tell them apart?"

Finn Boyle turns on his stool. "Hey you, back there! Shut the fuck up!"

Good God. This day is turning on me, it's doing the old one-eighty. That squished-name dog meat cost me sixty dollars, I've got a hundred left, plus Anna's fifty, but it's disappearing like water down the drain.

When who should return but Anna herself, another symbol of my declining stock, another reminder that while other people still think I have some value in the world — including this bright, vibrant, long-legged, beautiful woman — I don't.

I personally don't believe I have any value in the world. Self-pitying as it may sound, it's true. And I would like to be allowed to sink back into that simple self-pity — just sit here at the bar, a fresh beer and a shot of Bushmills in front of me — but I can't because here she comes, bearing down on me with that powerful sense of self she possesses, that conviction that the world is her oyster, and that I am but one tiny pearl on the endless necklace of her life.

"Darling!" she calls. "Wonderful news!"

I turn like a caged animal to face my keeper. I try to smile. "You came back. *Quelle surprise encore.*"

Since our last encounter, she's changed her clothing — or gone out and bought herself a new outfit. To help her forget our little spat, I suppose. A brown leather bomber jacket and a Yankees cap. No question about it — she's a knockout.

"The Gauguin exhibit? The one that's in Chicago? It was supposed to go to Vancouver next, but there was some kind of flap and it's coming here instead! In January! Isn't that marvellous?"

"Marvellous." I can't look at her. She's everything I'm not. She's many things I used to be. I turn away from her and stare at my hands on the bar.

"Darling," she says, and she's up close to me now, "come with me."

"Sure," I say to my ashtray. "I've always liked those Tahitian paintings. Not to mention those Titian paintings."

"No, now," she says. "I want you to come with me now."

I continue to gaze at my ashtray. "Where?"

"Anywhere but here. This place is no good for you, don't you see that? Come with me. We'll go shopping and buy you some decent clothes and get you a haircut and we'll have dinner at Pronto and then we'll go see whatever they've replaced *Phantom* with. I've told you about my friend, Kyle? All I have to do is give him a call, and the tickets will be waiting for us at the box office. Oh, it's a perfect idea, I'm so proud of myself for thinking it up. Come with me. Say you will."

I feel like I did when my mother dressed me for Sunday school in itchy grey flannels and starchy white shirts. All I wanted to do was stay in my room and read comics. Or like I did when I hit puberty and she made me go to Young People's Club. Girls with moustaches and armpit stains. Didn't know enough to keep their legs shut when they were sitting on the sofas. I didn't want to go then and I don't want to go now. "No thanks, baby, I'm happy here. I'll just stay put."

"Darling," Anna says, with a note of warning in her voice.

"I'm happy here," I repeat, raising my eyes to the middle distance that hovers over the tiers of bottles — the Sauza, the Kahlua, the Johnny Walker Red.

"Darling," she says again.

"Please go away," I plead. "Just leave me alone."

"I'm not going to put up with this. I have a life, you know, which is more than I can say for you, and I'm tired of being ignored when we're together. Sometimes I don't think you care a whit about me."

I keep looking at the bottles — the Sauza, the Kahlua.

"Look at me," she says.

But I can't. "Please leave me alone."

A few seconds later I feel the wash of light from the street that signals her departure.

"Dexter," I say. "Bushmills, please."

* * *

One time, when I was still pretty new to the racing business, I was sent to cover a meet at Fairmount Park in Collinsville, Illinois, just across the Mississippi from St. Louis. I was pretty lonely there, like I am now, actually, but I wasn't as used to it then, and most nights I ended up at a place called The Brickyards, in East St. Louis. I hadn't really started drinking heavily yet, but I suppose that's where it started. There, or at one of the other B-tracks I worked at. Or all of them combined.

One evening there was a wedding reception in the banquet room of The Brickyards. To get to the banquet room, the guests had to pass by the end of the bar where I was sitting. After an hour or two I was on a nodding acquaintance with some of them, including the groom, a burly kid about twenty with a blond crewcut, his red bow tie undone and dangling, and the top of his fancy red shirt open. At some point I told him congratulations, and he laid his hand on my shoulder and invited me to join the festivities.

Inside the banquet room the DJ was playing Neil Diamond, and everyone was dancing and singing along. They all knew the words and they all knew each other. It was like a grad dance, and everyone was drunk and happy.

The groom introduced me to his bride, who was petite and drop-dead gorgeous. Big brown eyes. I don't think she was overly glad to have me crash her wedding reception, but at the end of the night when everyone but me had left and her husband was so hammered he could barely stand up, she asked me to help her get him to the car. With one of his arms around each of our necks, we staggered to the parking lot where a gleaming black '64 Chevy Impala convertible was waiting. Top down, white interior. She asked me if I would drive them to their motel. I wasn't exactly sober myself, but we piled in — the bride beside me, the groom in the backseat howling "Sweeeeet Care-o-line!" I followed her directions out to a mom-and-pop motel on the highway. They didn't have a reservation, which seemed odd to me for a wedding night. Later when I thought back on it, I remembered noticing how the guests at the reception weren't dressed up at all, just the sort of clothes you'd wear to a picnic or a pool party, all of which suggested to me that the wedding itself was spur-of-the-moment.

The bride asked me if I would get them a room. She came into the office with me — she was still in her wedding dress — and even though the desk clerk looked at us suspiciously, he let us register. Because I didn't know the groom's full name — his first name was Brad — I signed my own. By the time we got back outside, Brad had struggled out of the backseat and was leaning on one of the fins at the rear of the car. I walked up to him to see if he was all right, and he grabbed my right hand with his left and hung on tight, like a little boy, and spewed his wedding feast all over the asphalt. The bride got some Kleenex out of the car and wiped his mouth, and again we supported him between us as we made our way towards the room. The desk clerk stepped out of his office into a pool of light and watched us, but he didn't say anything, and the bride and I grinned at each other over the back of her husband's neck. We propped him beside the door to the room, and while I fiddled with the key she leaned into him like a flying buttress, her arms like ramrods, her hands against his chest, her head down between her shoulders, her feet spread for balance in their little white satin slippers, and him hiccoughing and telling her how much he loved her.

We got him onto the bed and he immediately began to snore. The bride removed his shoes and dropped them on the floor. She went into the bathroom, and when she emerged a few minutes later, she was still in her wedding dress. She lay down beside her husband, reached over to turn out the bedside lamp, and saw me standing by the door like a cigar store Indian. "Sleep on the couch," she said. "Don't worry, it's all right." I had no idea how to get back to my car at The Brickyards anyway, and I was pretty much broke by this point — I had no money for a cab — so I stayed. Of course, if I'd really wanted to I could have found a way back to my car, but the fact of the matter was I didn't want to. I was as happy as I'd ever been in my life. I loved these people.

But in the morning the grey-faced groom didn't know who I was. He didn't know why I was there. As she'd done the night before, the bride took charge. She explained everything to him, soothingly, and he shook my hand. They drove me back to my car. It was about ten o'clock. At the bride's invitation, I followed them to a little park. We sat at a picnic table and drank Coca-Cola. After awhile the groom went off to buy pizza slices. While he was gone, the bride moved around to my side of the table and sat beside me. For a moment I thought she was going to make a pass at me, but I couldn't have been more wrong. She was all business. She looked me hard in the eyes and said, "Day after tomorrow, he's going to Vietnam. This is all the time we've got."

The party was over, and I'd been too stupid to catch on. That's always been one of my faults — staying too long at the party, suddenly looking around and discovering I'm the only one left, except for some joker out cold under the coffee table with chip dip on his shirt. Me with a lampshade on my head. The host and hostess gone to bed.

I gave her my mailing address, and she gave me theirs.

When her husband came back with the pizza slices, I ate quickly, said my goodbyes, and drove away with a lump in my throat.

A month or so later, I wrote a letter to the bride. If I remember correctly, the address she'd given me was in Pine Lawn, Missouri. I asked about her husband and what news she'd received, if any. I think I kind of fantasized that I could be a support to her while he was gone. A couple of weeks later my letter came back. *Nobody here by that name*, someone had scrawled across the envelope.

Here's Tommy Belyea hoving into view, hangdog and haggard. The poor boy. He walks right up to where I'm sitting. "Have you seen my mother?" he asks, eyes downcast, a tremor in his voice.

I try to think, but I can't remember when I last saw her. "She hasn't been in here for a while, Tommy."

"I took her home and made her something to eat," he says, "and she seemed fine, and I put *Oprah* on for her, and then I went into my room and had Tom Waits on, but not so loud I couldn't hear the TV over it, but all of a sudden I couldn't hear the TV, so I go back out to the living room, and she's gone." He shakes his head, and then his chin begins to wobble. "She turned the TV off, but she left the door wide open."

Jessy's placed a rolled-up paper napkin in front of me. I slide the knife and fork out and hand the napkin to Tommy, who dabs his eyes with it. "I don't know what I'm going to do, Mr. Harvey. I can't look after her. One day she'll get lost, or run over, or who knows." He honks his nose into the napkin. "I better try the fire hall."

I watch him go, then swivel back around. Dexter's standing there watching the door swing shut. "While you're up," I say to him, "I'll have a pint."

Dexter nods at a nearly full glass eight inches from my nose. "I believe that's yours right there," he says.

Beside me, Finn Boyle says, "Who's the kid?"

I lean my head into my hands and massage my temples with my thumbs. "He lives in my building. His mother's got Alzheimer's."

"And the tall drink of water? Who was she?"

I breathe deeply before I answer. "Anna."

"What's her story?"

"I used to be her flavour of the week. For a while there. But I think maybe she's ready to move on." I smile like it's nothing, but my hand, as I reach for my pint, shakes like a leaf. "I think I'll get some air."

It's getting dark out and it's started to snow. I look down and there's slush on my shoes. I came outside because I was getting fucked up inside, but things aren't any better out here. Dusk fucks me up. Early winter fucks me up. Bad weather fucks me up.

I have my highs and lows like everybody else. Simple things make me happy. Giving Zontar an answer for the trivia game. Picking a winner. But when I do win I usually ruin it by wishing I'd bet more than I did — but so what, every gambler does that.

The carpet always seems to get pulled out from under the things that make me happy. I want to hope for the best, but I always end up expecting the worst. Somebody told me once that a cynic is nothing more than a disillusioned idealist, a lapsed romantic, someone who never gets over the shock of discovering that the bad guys win at least as much, maybe even more, than the good guys do. I guess that's what I am: a lapsed romantic.

Barbara used to tell me I have a depressive personality. The first time she shared this weighty insight with me, we were having dinner at our favourite steakhouse before going to one of those musicals she couldn't get enough of. That's one thing she and Anna have in common: culture. Art galleries and concerts and plays. If I got home from work before she did, and among the bills and junk mail on the floor inside the front door there was a flyer from one of these theatre companies promoting its upcoming production of *Oklahoma!* or *The Iceman Cometh*, I'd toss it in the trash before she caught sight of it, thereby saving myself a long boring evening watching wannabe Brandos and Hepburns prancing around a makeshift stage in a renovated church in a rundown part of the city.

Anyway, I'd probably had too much wine, I *know* I'd had too much wine, and it must have been late fall, November maybe, just like now, because I was going on about how I hated the thought of winter.

"You have a depressive personality," Barbara told me. "You let things get you down. For instance, you always get depressed when the seasons change."

"I do?"

"Yes, you do. You may hate the thought of winter, but you hate the thought of spring, too."

"That's not true, I *love* spring."

She shakes her head. "All the dog turds you find on the

front lawn after the snow melts. All the trash — cigarette butts and bottle caps and candy wrappers."

I nodded. "I stand corrected, you're right, I do hate spring. What about summer? Do I hate summer, too?"

"Of course. You hate the arrival of every season. Because it never lives up to what it's supposed to be. Spring's supposed to symbolize rebirth, right? But all you notice is that our noisy neighbours, who've been silent all winter because they were cooped up inside their house, are outside again, drinking beer and barbequing and arguing with each other at the tops of their lungs. In summer, I think it's the bugs that get to you the most. Mosquitoes and blackflies and earwigs and those awful things with all the legs that crawl out of drains. And you're always complaining about people's lawnmowers and power tools. And their music. Car radios. Boom boxes in people's backyards. What is it our neighbours are always playing? Rap?"

"Yeah, all that hip hop crap."

"Right. Well, your music's almost as bad. At least they haven't discovered jazz yet. Priam, do you have any idea how crazy, how frenetic, *your* music makes me?"

"What about the fall? Why do I hate the fall?"

She looked at me like I was thick. "Because it comes before winter. If winter symbolizes old age and death, then the fall symbolizes middle age. Am I right? Spring is youth. Summer, we're in our prime. Fall is middle age, *late* middle age. The leaves fall. Your hair falls out."

"'Bare ruin'd choirs,'" I intoned, "'where late the sweet birds sang.'"

She glanced at her wristwatch. "Oh, Christ. Finish your wine. Get the waiter. We're going to be late, and then they won't let us in till there's a lull, and then we'll have to squeeze past an entire gauntlet of really indignant people."

I wanted to keep talking. I wanted to talk about my depressive personality, and I wanted to talk about people with other types of personality that depress me — drivers who deposit the contents of their ashtrays on the pavement before they pull out of their parking spaces; garbagemen who won't collect your garbage unless it's presented properly; chimney cleaners who phone at suppertime to warn you that if you don't hire them to clean your chimney there's a good chance you and your family will asphyxiate during your sleep — but instead I concentrated on how to finish the half-glass of wine in front of me plus the last two inches in the bottle without appearing to the waiters or the diners at the surrounding tables to be a man with a drinking problem. I wasn't worried about Barbara: she already knew I had a drinking problem.

For me, the only thing worse than being a drunk or a drug addict would be if I were the father of one. I think of Campbell Young and the difficulties he had with Debi, his daughter, and I know it would have been more than I could bear to see her change from the sweet little girl she was to the stranger she became — ruled by television and peer pressure, disfigured by tattoos and tongue studs. I wouldn't have been able to bear the nights she didn't come home, the glazed eyes when she did, the horrible music pumping through the walls, the door to her room shut tighter than a crack den, the windows of the cars her boyfriends picked her up in tinted so that I couldn't see what they looked like — their bling, their hats on sideways. I wouldn't have been able to bear the phone call from the police — or no phone call at all, as happened with Shannon Brown. Eight years and still no word.

Happily — for her sake and her father's — Debi straightened herself out. She's a good mom and she works hard.

Nevertheless, I'm glad I never had a daughter. I wouldn't have known what to say to her or how to handle her. I wouldn't have been able to look after her. The truth is I was a failure as a father. My son grew up in the Bahamas, and I never really knew him. To have lost a child I did know would have been the end of me.

The slush on my shoes is leaking through. My feet feel cold and damp. Or maybe I'm imagining they do. My sense of touch, like most of my senses, is not as sharp as it once was.

I look across the street at the old racetrack. The floodlights are on, so that even after dark the wrecking machines continue their work. The investors must be growing antsy: they're keen to get the new subdivision started, to begin the process of selling unbuilt condos for preposterous amounts of money.

A shiver runs up my neck. I'm about to turn and go back into the bar when a car pulls up in front of me at the curb. The passenger window lowers, and a young woman leans her head out and says, "Hey, mister, can you help us?"

I incline my head slightly. She appears to be East Indian. "Are you lost?"

"We just need some directions." She laughs. "Come closer, I won't bite."

I step forward and lean into the window, my hands on the sill. She has black hair to her shoulders and black, almond-shaped eyes. In the subdued light of the dashboard her skin is mahogany, dark mahogany with highlights of underwater green — deep-sea green. Sitting beside her in the driver's seat is the boy with the turban. He's smoking a cigarette and fiddling with the radio. He doesn't look at me. I straighten up and step back. I hadn't even noticed it was the black Acura.

"Hey, don't go away," the girl says. "I told Nasir to stop because I thought you looked, like, so totally attractive in your white suit, and I wanted to talk to you. We don't really need directions. I just said that. I thought maybe someone interesting-looking like you might want some company. I know I would enjoy *your* company, big time. What's your name? I bet you have a real dignified name, like George or Henry. Mine's Tahira, and if you got any problems, I'm not saying you do, but if you got any problems, I can make them go away. I can make them disappear. I got a room upstairs, it's clean —"

"Here?"

"Yes, right here at the Hearth&Home."

I look across the road at the destruction of the racetrack. "How much?" I ask.

"Depends what you want. A blow job's fifty, but we park down the street for that. Two hundred you can fuck me, plus we go to the room, which is included in the price. And I provide the condom. But no kissing on the mouth. You can kiss me other places, but not on the mouth."

Her voice has changed. The seduction's gone. If she wasn't ravishingly beautiful, she could be Judy, at Ginger's, reciting the specials.

"So what do you say?"

I look back down at her, then do a slow vertical pan past the Acura's gleaming black roof, past the wreckage of the racetrack, and up into the night sky. What with the yellow glare from the floodlights I can't tell whether it's overcast or clear, and if it's clear, whether there are any stars out.

"No, thank you," I say.

"Let's go," Tahira says.

Nasir puts the car in gear, and as they squeal away from the curb, the Acura's Michelins spray slush onto my pantlegs.

I'm still standing there when Campbell Young approaches along the sidewalk, pushing his friend Arthur Trick in his wheelchair.

"Who was that?" Young asks, puffing.

"Young lady of Asian persuasion," I tell him, "who thought I was hot." I nod at Arthur. "Good to see you, Arthur. How are you keeping?"

"Fair to middling, and you, Mr. Harvey?"

"Fine, thank you."

Young says, "Yeah, well, I'm not fine."

"I was just about to ask —"

"I don't know how there can be anything left inside me seeing as how I've been on the shitter so many times in the past twelve hours my asshole feels like somebody's been at it with a wire brush. Bad guys show up yet?"

"No," I say, "all quiet so far."

"Good," he says. "Didn't want to miss out on the action. Come on, let's get inside before we freeze our asses off."

NINTH RACE

POST TIME: 4:52 P.M.

(6 FURLONGS.
THE "GLORY GIRL" STAKES.
3-YEAR-OLD FILLIES, CANADIAN-FOALED.
PURSE $125,000 ADDED.)

1 WEB SITE
2 EUROPA
3 FESTIVE
4 SNUGGLE
5 PLAIN QUEEN
6 OFF BY HEART
7 CHINA GIRL
8 BINGO DAUGHTER
9 TENDERLY
10 SHOWY
11 SUN HAT
12 HARRY'S ROSE

Soon after Campbell Young has situated Arthur at a table near the karaoke stage and I've returned to my stool at the corner of the bar, I feel his heavy hand on my shoulder. "So, Mr. Harvey," he says, "why did you call me instead of calling the cops? I *used* to work for the city, but I don't anymore. I'm retired from that, as you well know. Now I work for jealous husbands who think their wife's fucking the tennis pro."

"Retirement's just a state of mind, right?" I say, looking up at him. "Besides, I thought you'd want to help out."

Young scans the room. "I do, but I don't see any problem. I'm looking at Dexter right now, and he looks just fine to me."

"Like I said outside," I tell him, "it's all quiet so far, but when those two boys show up — and they will — there's going to be trouble. But maybe you'd like a second opinion. Maybe you should have a word with Dexter, get his perspective on the situation."

Young lifts his chin. When he's towering over you it's like sitting at the foot of a cliff, gazing up at the brink. His shirt collar must be a twenty. He watches Dexter getting in the face of a guy in a Red Sox cap, then frowns down on me from that spectacular height of his. "Okay," he says, "I'll talk to him."

"What he needs is a word to the wise," I say. "He needs to hear it from you that this whole thing could turn out badly."

"Then that's what I'll do. I'll have a word with Dexter. But as you can see he's busy at the moment, so me and Trick are going to have a beer first, as served by the lovely Jessy, and some chicken wings — the hot ones, I imagine, of which Trick is especially fond of."

"You really think you should be eating spicy food with your stomach the way it is?"

"Fuck it, I can't feel any worse. Besides which, I'm pretty sure Trick's already ordered them, and besides which, I haven't eaten anything since last night and I'm starved."

* * *

The ninth is the stakes race, and Kelvin Chan's filly, Off by Heart, is as close to a sure thing as I'm likely to see in this lifetime. She won't be the chalk — which is a good thing — but she'll win, and if I bet my last hundred on her, I'll be able to look myself in the eye — this would be via the cracked, yellowing mirror on the door of the medicine chest in the cubbyhole that passes for a bathroom in my furnished room at the Everdon — and say to myself, "Yes, my friend, you are indeed and always have been and always will be — despite your share of knock-downs along the road of life and despite the women who have mistaken you for a loser — a man of substance."

Beside me, Finn Boyle says, "Who do you like in here?" He's leaning his head forward on an angle so that his good eye can scan the entries for the ninth race in my *Form*.

"The six," I tell him, "is a lock."

Jessy appears and places a large plate bearing a burger and salad in front of me. I'd forgotten I'd ordered them.

She drops a small plate of fries in front of Finn Boyle. "Ah, Jessy," he says. "Did you miss me while I was away?"

"Were you away?" she says.

"Yes, I was away."

"Where to?"

"Up the river."

"Up the river, and now you're back I'm supposed to get all wet?"

Finn Boyle turns to me. "Girl's still got a mouth on her." He looks back at Jessy. "You remember me," he says, and the humour's gone out of his voice. "I'm Irish, like you are. We both have people in Dublin."

"And your name would be …?"

"You know my name."

"I may have at one time," she says, her voice deadly, "but I don't now. Anyway, I only have eyes for Mr. Harvey." She flashes them at me. "Isn't that right, Mr. Harvey?" Then she's gone.

Finn Boyle narrows his eyes at me. "Bastard," he says evenly. "You got something going with her?"

I laugh, but I watch him carefully. This could be a dangerous moment, one of those moments that erupt between two men who've been drinking together for hours and appear to everyone around them to be old pals, buying each other beers, arms around each other's shoulders. One of those moments when one man breaks a bottle against the edge of a table and grinds it in the other man's face.

His lower lip juts out and he glares at me one-eyed, head tilted. Then he nods his head quickly and to the side, with a twist almost. "Buy me a shot of your whiskey," he says.

"You haven't finished your Duck Fart."

He glances at the mud-coloured drink in front of him, then back at me. "Buy me a shot of your whiskey."

"Dexter," I say, without taking my eyes off Finn Boyle, "a Bushmills for my friend here. And a Bud, too, please, for the slake-throated Dale."

Finn Boyle says, "I love whiskey. It either makes me want to fuck or fight."

"Or both?" I say, getting off my stool.

"Yeah, sometimes both. Where're you going?"

"Place a bet."

"Wait," he says, and pulls a folded fifty-dollar bill out of his shirt pocket. "On the nose. Number six."

"Here I've been buying you food and drink, and you've

been holding out on me. Turns out you're a rich man."

"See what a sap you are."

Dexter delivers the whiskey and the Budweiser. I thank him, then take Finn Boyle's money and the bottle of beer and make my way through the crowd. It's almost suppertime, and people are arriving for the Wednesday night ten-cents-a-wing special. The air is thick with smoke, and people are not exactly shouting, but their volume's up so they can be heard over a karaoke singer who's doing her best to sound like Whitney Houston. Panther and the twins are huddled over Panther's *Form* at the island, and as Jessy brushes past me with a basket of wings and a pitcher of beer, she says, "Walk a girl home, Mr. Harvey? I'm off early. Eight o'clock."

I pull up short. "What about your rule?"

She leans close to my ear and whispers loudly, huskily, "I know, and I'm a person of my word, but if you remember, we never did it. You fell asleep, and we never even did it. So I think that's grounds for an exception to the rule. D' you agree?"

I step back and look at her, and a bit of light catches the green of her eyes. "I agree, yes, definitely."

She nods and hurries away.

I'd better go easy on the drinking, I think, as I push my way through to Dale. I want to be in condition. Too much booze is bad for the boudoir. I want to be able to drive to the wire, not limp home exhausted. Played out. Spent.

"Dale," I say when I reach him, "a hundred to win — including fifty for Finn Boyle — fifty to place and fifty to show on the six."

"Are you trying to kill me?" he says.

"Hey, don't take it if it's too much."

"Just kidding, my friend. A hundred, fifty, fifty on the six."

I place two hundred dollars on his tray — my hundred, Finn Boyle's fifty, and — may God have mercy on my soul — Anna's fifty. Other people are lining up behind me to do business with him, so without ceremony I hand him the Budweiser, and on my way back to the bar I see Campbell Young waving at me. His fingers are orange with chicken wing sauce. Next to them on the little karaoke stage Zontar has just launched into "Ain't Nothing Like the Real Thing."

"I saw you making a bet with Dale," Young says. "Any information you'd care to share?"

"I have it on good authority that the six will win the feature. In fact, I'd say it was a sure thing, and that's not something I say cavalierly."

"A sure thing, eh? Sure things make me nervous. Who's your good authority?"

"Normally I wouldn't reveal my sources — old rule of journalism — but in this case I see no reason not to: Kelvin Chang."

Arthur says, "Trainer, right?"

"Right."

Young wipes his fingers on a napkin and gets to his feet.

"Have you talked to Dexter yet?" I ask.

"When I'm done eating," he says, and heads off towards Dale.

"Count me in," Arthur calls after him.

Back at the bar, Finn Boyle's inhaled his fries and gravy, and now he's eyeing my burger. I slide the plate away from him. "Did you know your old favourite ran this afternoon?"

I turn the pages of the *Form* back to the third race. "See? Number eight."

Finn Boyle's gaze shifts from my dinner to my *Form*. He leans his head close to the page. "Red Scout? Red Scout ran today and I wasn't here! Goddamn it to hell! How'd he do?"

"He won. Last to first. His usual modus operandi. Won by a length."

"What odds?"

"Eight to one."

Finn Boyle's head falls forward into his hands. "I would've been all over that bet! That fifty I just gave you? It'd be four-fifty now, goddamn it." He turns his head and swivels his good eye up at me, like a gecko, and smiles. "You're just fucking with me, aren't you? He finished up the track. Am I right? You're just having a little fun at my expense."

I shake my head and point to the top right corner of the page in my *Form* where I wrote down the payoffs. "Look. Eighteen-twenty to win, eight even to place, four-fifty to show."

He lifts his head from the bar but his face has gone serious. "Did you bet him?"

"Yes, I bet him."

"Heavy?"

"Five across, Finn, that's all. In your honour. Ask Dale. 'For Finn Boyle,' I said. 'For old times' sake.'"

His face lights up again. "You bet for me?"

I can see where this is headed. "In your *honour*, Finn. It's not your money. It's my money. I had no idea you were going to show up today, did I?"

"But it was Red Scout. I always bet Red Scout."

"But you weren't here to bet it —"

"Exactly, and you bet it for me, in my honour, because

you're my friend." He grasps my wrist. "How much did I make?"

I look up at TV #1. "The horses are in the gate," I tell him. "Don't forget you've got fifty on the six." I check the odds at the side of the screen. "She's three to one. That's very good value."

Finn Boyle looks up at the screen. "What's her name again?"

"Off by Heart."

The gate opens and the horses break well except for Off by Heart, who stumbles and almost goes to her knees. Her jockey gathers her quickly, and in no time she's flying down the backstretch, passing horses — it's a field of twelve — and midway through the far turn she's only four lengths off the leaders, five fillies spread out in front of her like a phalanx. Into the stretch she's full of run, but there's no opening through the wall in front of her. Just when I'm thinking the jockey will take her outside and risk losing ground, a small hole opens between the horse on the rail and the one next to her, and the jockey drives for the hole, hand-riding, in too close to use the whip, and I close my eyes for a second, Finn Boyle beside me pounding the bar with his fists and shouting, "Come *on*, you six! Come *on*, you six!" and when I open them again, she's through the hole and clear, and sprints away in the last thirty yards, drawing away from the others like they're standing still.

"Going away!" I yell. "Oh baby!" My hands are shaking, but I feel so good I have to yell again. "Oh baby, yes! Thank you, Kelvin, thank you!" I'm still watching her gallop out, and I'm slapping Finn Boyle on the back, and Finn Boyle's just sitting there stunned, and I'm thinking fifty dollars at three to one is two hundred, plus the place and show bets will gross somewhere in the neighbourhood of four hundred, maybe a little less, but who's counting, when the TV screen cuts to the tote board, and the INQUIRY sign and the numbers of the win, place, and show horses — 6, 12, 3 — start flashing.

"What the hell?" I say.

I turn to Finn Boyle — my hand's still on his shoulder — and he says, "She's coming down."

"What? Why?"

"Weren't you watching the goddamn race?" he says. "She barreled between horses like a fucking fullback. She slammed both of them. She's coming down."

The TV cuts to a slow motion profile shot of the stretch run, and you can see the five horses abreast, a grey on the outside, the rest all bays, and then you can see the chestnut Off by Heart behind them, and then watch her driving for the hole, and then she's through like a shot and starts distancing them. "I saw one jock come up a bit in the irons," I say, "but that's all. I didn't see anything."

"She's coming down," Finn Boyle says.

The screen cuts to the tote board, and the INQUIRY sign is still flashing. Then another slow-motion replay begins, this time from head-on, the horses running straight at us.

"Watch," Finn Boyle says.

The five horses charging towards the camera seem to be running in place, making no progress, the puffs of dirt at their hooves mere illusions of motion. They're so close together I can't see Off by Heart behind them. The grey on the left of the screen, the four bays shoulder to shoulder beside her, one with a big star on her forehead, one with blue blinkers. A gap slowly grows between the two horses on the rail, and there's Off by Heart — her gold coat gleaming, her white blaze bobbing — surging into the gap, then the filly on her outside bounces off her and bodychecks the filly next to her while the filly on the inside hits the rail so hard her jockey has to stand up to get her under control.

"Oh fuck," I say.

The INQUIRY sign stops flashing and goes solid, the numbers of the three horses vanish, and a few seconds later the OFFICIAL sign appears. A few more seconds and the numbers come up: 12, 3, 10.

"They didn't just take her down," Finn Boyle says. "We're off the fucking board."

"What's this 'we'?" I say. "You didn't bet place and show. *I* bet place and show. You lost fifty dollars, I lost a hundred and fifty!"

"Well, you don't have to get all fucked up about it!"

I swivel on my stool and look over to the island. No sign of Ronny and Harry. Maybe they've left. Then I look over towards Dale, and there they are — ready to collect. Panther's with them, pumping his fist in the air.

I turn and look back up at the screen. The twelve horse, Harry's Rose, pays $26.40 to win. Harry's Rose. Of course. How could I have missed it? Hunch fucking bettors, I hate the fucking bastards.

Another long shot, Festive, who finished third, is placed second. The favourite, Showy, moves up from fourth to third. The exactor pays three hundred and change.

I take my wallet out of my hip pocket and peer inside. One lousy fin. I search my pants pockets and come up with three dollars in change. Eight dollars to my name.

"Dexter," I say.

"Yes, Mr. Harvey?"

"Once again I discover that I'm financially embarrassed.

I'll have to put today's expenses on account, I'm afraid."

Dexter says nothing. He reaches under the bar and produces a ledger. He opens it, flips through it until he finds the page he's looking for, studies it, and says, "It's only the tenth of the month, Mr. Harvey, and you already owe a hundred and sixty-two dollars and eighty-five cents. Not including today."

The twins are back at the island, laughing, Panther stuck to them like a barnacle.

"Mr. Harvey? I said you already owe —"

"Thank you, Dexter, I heard you."

Fucking hunch bettors. I get a legitimate tip, I've got the best horse in the race, she deserves to win, she *does* win, but her number comes down, and Panther and those two assholes he's taken up with in their Perry Como sweaters win on a fucking hunch. Somebody get me a gun.

I look up at TV #1. The entries for the tenth are up. The ninth is over, it's history. Kelvin's filly won and then she lost. I lost a hundred and a half, including Anna's fifty. Finn Boyle lost fifty. I have no idea how much Campbell Young and Arthur lost. I look over at their table. A woman wearing a cowboy hat is sitting in Young's chair talking to Arthur; Young's nowhere in sight — probably on the crapper again. Kelvin must have lost a pile, too. And now I've got eight dollars to my name, and a ballooning tab. A mushroom cloud of a tab. Well, that's the way it goes, right? That's horse racing.

My eyes slide past the trivia question on TV #2 — all I catch is WHICH OF THE FOLLOWING COUNTRIES — and come to rest on Shannon Brown's eyes staring out of TV #3. Eyes no more. Eyes no more than little ghost eyes.

And there she is at sixteen. Or rather someone's prediction of what she would look like at sixteen. Is one photo more real than the other? Neither photo is real, of course, any more than she is. Once upon a time she was real, but my money says all that came to an end a long time ago on a dirt road somewhere outside of Beaverton. Staring out from the ghostly line of trees, the line of ghostly trees, two little ghost eyes.

What about the bastard that took her? Is he still alive? Maybe he killed himself. Blew his brains out in a fit of self-loathing. Or knelt in front of a train, or jumped off a bridge — a cinder block roped to his neck. Or is he still stalking little girls? Little girls who smile into the camera. Little girls who trust —

"Excuse me for bothering you, Mr. Harvey, but have you by any chance seen Tommy?" I turn to my left, towards the sound of Mrs. Belyea's voice — I didn't know she was back in the bar — but beyond her — beyond the peroxide flash of her hair, the scarlet slash of her lipstick — I see them moving quickly in my direction: Mr. Clean, a black look in his eyes, his right hand inside his trench coat, and behind him Short Eyes.

Mr. Clean pushes past Mrs. Belyea, who says, "I *beg* your pardon!"

His hand emerges from his coat.

The scissors he's holding are large, like sewing shears.

Everything slows to a crawl. Voices take on an echo.

I turn towards Dexter. He's got his back to us — he's got a paper plate in one hand, and with the other he's fishing in the jar of pickled eggs with a pair of tongs.

Beside me, Finn Boyle's off his stool. He lifts his walking stick and holds it above his head, horizontally. "Who the fuck are you?" he demands, his voice as slow as cement. "You'd better get the fuck out of here —"

"That's it!" Short Eyes shouts, and the slow motion

snaps back to normal speed, fast speed, and Short Eyes shouts, "That's what the nigger hit me with!" and Mr. Clean, scissors raised in his right hand, kicks Finn Boyle in the crotch with his right foot — a straight-leg kick, as if he were kicking a field goal — and Finn Boyle squeals and goes down. Mr. Clean turns and steps towards me, and I swivel around and lay my head on my forearms on the bar. He's right beside me, I can smell his rotten smell. His hand is on the back of my neck, and I can feel panic coming on like paralysis, but just as quickly he's gone, and when I lift my head he's clambering over the bar, scattering ashtrays and Bits & Bites and my burger platter and *Racing Forms* and draft glasses, and Dexter's facing us now and backing up against the tiers of bottles, and the Smirnoff topples, and the Wild Turkey. Beside me, Short Eyes is standing over Finn Boyle, kicking him in the ribs, and down on the floor Finn Boyle says "Oof!" each time he's kicked.

I put my forehead back down on the bar and place my hands over my ears, but I can still hear Mr. Clean. "Come here, Sambo," he bellows, "I got something for you! Come here, Sambo!"

I twist my head and peek under my arm.

Panther is standing at the island with his mouth open.

Beneath the island, the twins crouch.

Zontar disappears into the crowd, suspenders flashing.

The woman in the cowboy hat turns to look.

Trick's looking, too.

I climb down off my stool and pick it up by two of its legs and lift it high over my head. I turn towards Short Eyes, who's still methodically kicking Finn Boyle, and bring the stool down on his head. Short Eyes falls to the floor beside Finn Boyle. As I'm setting the stool back on its feet, Short

Eyes struggles to his hands and knees. Panther steps around the island and drops on him like a lineman on a fumble. I pick up Finn Boyle's walking stick and turn towards the bar, but I can't get to Mr. Clean from where I am, so I walk to the end of the bar where the cash register is and where Jessy's holding a basket of wings in one hand and a pitcher of beer in the other and screaming. I ease past her and go behind the bar where I've never been before, to where Mr. Clean's got Dexter up against the cigarette display, the tips of the scissor blades to Dexter's throat, and I raise the walking stick in both my hands, like an axe, and bring it down on the side of Mr. Clean's head. He turns and looks at me and he's got that dead look in his eyes, that killer look I noticed the first time I saw him, and I raise the walking stick again, and he turns away just before I bring it down, but I catch him solidly on the back of the head, and the orange hair there goes dark where the blood begins to pump out in gouts, and he swings around towards me again and shakes his head, and I hear the spray of blood spatter on the bar, and then he takes a step towards me and I take a step backwards and he pitches forward on his face, and the scissors clatter out of his hand, and I sweep them behind me with my foot towards the cash register where Jessy's still screaming, and Dexter gives me this flare-eyed look like he's staring at a madman, and I feel shaky all of a sudden, as if I might pass out again, so I sit down on the floor, and what do I see on the shelf under the bar, beside a jug of Clamato? My bottle of Bushmills. Staring right at me. I reach for it, but I'm shaking too much to grasp it. Not just my hand. My whole arm. So I lean back against the bar fridge. My heart's pounding, and all I can hear is my breathing.

But then I'm aware of a voice above me, on the other

side of the bar. "Aren't you the young man I spoke with earlier? It's Chris, isn't it?" The voice is distant, but I can hear it plainly. The sound is soothing, and I close my eyes to listen. "You haven't by any chance seen my Tommy, have you? He's supposed to walk Pepper, but I can't find him anywhere. He must be off with his friends somewhere, and I'm afraid she can't wait much longer. I just talked to Dorothy, John's secretary, and she said he'll be along as soon as he can. And I spoke to Mr. Harvey just a moment ago ... where *is* Mr. Harvey?"

"You okay, Mr. Harvey?" Campbell Young says. He's looming over me, doing up his belt.

"I'm all right."

"I was standing here just a minute ago," he says, "waiting for Dexter to get me a pickled egg, but then I had to run to the shitter, and then I heard the commotion and came back as quick as I could" — he takes a look around — "but it doesn't look like you needed me." I follow the direction of his eyes to my right, and there's Mr. Clean, on his back now, his eyes open but rolled inside his head, nothing but the whites showing, and the ear near me's full of blood. His orange Chia Pet hair sickens me, and the red puddle under his head's still spreading. His lips are quivering, then, so loudly I jerk back, he says, "Get inside and fix my dinner!" He stops talking, but his lips are still moving frantically. Then, "You hear me, woman? Get inside the goddamn house, get the goddamn dinner on the goddamn table!" I look up at Dexter. He's holding Finn Boyle's walking stick and staring down at Mr. Clean. There's nothing in his eyes; the flare-eyed look he gave me earlier's gone. Now his eyes are as dead as Mr. Clean's. With the tipped end of the walking stick pressed against a cheekbone, he adjusts Mr. Clean's head so that his face is pointing skyward. Then, reversing the walking stick — knobbed end down — and holding it like a golf club, Dexter delivers a short, sharp blow to the temple. Mr. Clean doesn't say anything after that.

TENTH RACE

POST TIME: 5:21 P.M.

(5 1/2 FURLONGS. TURF.
4-YEAR-OLDS AND UP.
ALLOWANCES.
PURSE $62,000.)

1 WINGSPAN [NZ]
2 FOLKSY
3 EL GRAN LOBO [ARG]
4 PURSUIT
5 SONNY BE GOOD
6 TEMPLE BAR [IRE]
7 FLATLANDER
8 WELLESLEY [GB]
9 CLEAN LIVING

There's been a pulsing in my ears for some time now, a few minutes at least, but it seems to be going away. I can hear sirens in the distance. And talking. Excited talking, like people in a line-up before a movie. I look at my hand. There are specks of blood on it. It's still trembling, but not as much.

Panther's face appears above the bar. "You okay, Mr. Harvey?"

I look back down to my hand, outstretched in front of me, and will it to settle down, to steady. I switch my focus to the bottle of Bushmills. "Never better," I tell him. "How's Finn Boyle?"

Panther looks to his left. "He's back on his stool. Seems all right."

Then I hear Dexter's voice say, "Mr. Harvey?"

I look to my right at his hairless, chocolate-brown legs, his black Lycra shorts, then tip my head back until I can see his face.

He's looking down at me. "It might be a good idea for you to get up and go back to your stool before the cops get here."

I take a slow breath. "Is Mrs. Belyea all right?"

"Tommy's here. He's taking her home."

I look to my right. Mr. Clean is still on his back, facing me. His eyes are still open and rolled back in his head. Blood leaks from his nose.

The sirens are getting closer.

Dexter says, "You'd better get up."

"Who called the cops?"

"No idea."

"Couldn't we have handled this ourselves?"

"Too late now, they're on their way."

As I struggle to my feet I keep my eye on the Bushmills. Not so much out of longing — more as a candle in the window, a beacon in the night. Once I'm up, I'm a little woozy, but generally okay. I make my way down the inside of the bar, nod to the glassy-eyed Jessy, make a wide turn around the cash register, and squeeze between the crowd standing at the island — among them Zontar and the woman with the cowboy hat and the man in the **DEVIL'S DEMONS** jacket — and the people sitting on bar stools. Somebody pats me on the back, somebody else pumps my hand, and somebody who sounds a lot like Sean Connery says, "Good old lad, you're a good old lad."

Finn Boyle is indeed back on his stool, and as I climb shakily onto mine, he says, "There you are, for fucksake, I was wondering where you'd got to." One side of his face is beet red, and there's blood on his chin.

The sirens are very loud now. I look through the front window of the bar as a police car pulls up outside. Every second or so, its revolving yellow light flashes through the window. When I turn back to Finn Boyle, I watch his cheek turn orange, then red, then orange again.

The bar's swarming with police officers and ambulance attendants. Detectives Lynn Wheeler and Tony Barkas arrive. Short Eyes is led out to a cruiser in handcuffs. A stretcher has to be wheeled in behind the bar for Mr. Clean. To get to him, the promotional umbrella and its plastic table and chairs have to be moved. The ambulance attendants look grim. Maybe the bastard's dead.

Statements are taken from various people, including Dexter and Panther and Jessy. Wheeler leans against the bar beside me and asks if I'd be willing to give one. "I've got nothing to say," I tell her.

No sooner does she leave than Young takes her place. "Me and Trick," he says, "lost a bill each on that filly of yours."

"Join the club," I say. "I lost a bill and a half, Finn lost fifty, and I'm sure Kelvin's hurting, too. It was just bad luck."

"Bad ride, more like it. Trying to get through a hole

where there was no hole."

"Oh well, there's nothing for it now."

We're quiet for a moment, and I become aware that Young's staring at me, sort of scrutinizing me.

"What?" I say.

"Like I say," he says, "I was in the shitter and missed all the excitement, but people tell me you smashed a stool over the one guy's head and walloped the other guy with a cane. Your moment of glory, your fifteen minutes of fame, and I missed it."

"Fifteen minutes of insanity, more like it. Fifteen *seconds!*"

"What they're saying is you saved Dexter's life."

He waits for me to say something, but I just stare into the fresh Creemore Dexter has placed in front of me.

"You did, didn't you? You saved Dexter's life."

I turn my head and look up at him. "You know me, Campbell. How am I going to save someone else's life when I can't save my own?"

Young says, "Maybe the next time you climb down off that stool, you'll stay down. How long you been sitting there anyway? Isn't it time you climbed down for good, got back to your writing?"

"I'm done writing, I've told you that."

"Well, you're going to have to do something — you obviously can't make a living playing the ponies."

"What I need is a new profession."

"Like what?"

"I don't know. Bounty hunter, maybe. That seems to be a popular line of work these days. Or maybe I'll become an investigative consultant, like you. I've done some snooping in my time."

Young sighs. "Joke if you want, but I hate to see a smart man like you drink your life away. You were such a good writer about horse racing, you could probably write about anything you set your mind to."

"What do you know about writing?"

"Nothing. Nothing at all. Hell, I think *Peanuts* is great literature. But you do. You know lots about writing."

A few minutes later, Panther's beside me. "So, Mr. Harvey," he says, "are you really all right?"

"I'm fine."

He shakes his head. "That was amazing. *You* were amazing."

"I seem to recall you jumping in, too."

"Yes, I did." He thumps his chest like Tarzan. A moment passes before he says, "I've got a question for you."

My ears are throbbing again. "What kind of question?"

"What's your favourite racetrack?"

I shrug. "I don't know —"

"Saratoga?"

"Saratoga's nice, all right. Beautiful. But I've always had a special place in my heart for Belmont."

"I've never been there, but I was always under the impression that it was sort of ugly."

"No, not at all. It's majestic. And I'll tell you something else: I've seen some of the greatest horses of all time there. I was there for twenty-some runnings of the Belmont Stakes when I was a journalist, starting with Secretariat in 1973. I was there in '77 when Seattle Slew won the Triple Crown and again in '78 when Affirmed won it. I was there when Ruffian took that bad step in the match race with Foolish Pleasure. I was there in '89 when Easy Goer beat Sunday

Silence by eight lengths —"

"What are you doing next summer?"

"What?"

"What are you doing next summer?"

I scratch behind my ear. "I don't know what I'm doing next *week*."

"Want to go on a trip?"

I shake my head to clear it. "What are you talking about?"

"I'm asking if you'd like to go on a trip."

I look at him. "You want me to go on a trip? With you? Why would I do that? I don't even like you."

His face falls. "You don't?"

"All that rejoicing with the twins!"

Panther frowns. "I admit I got a little carried away, but that's no reason not to like someone."

"In my opinion it's plenty of reason."

"Well, I'm sorry, I —"

"What kind of trip?"

He takes a breath. "A road trip."

"A road trip. Where to?"

"Well, I've always wanted to tour the great racetracks of America. Maybe write a book about them."

"I thought you wrote poetry."

"I write other things, too."

"And now you want to write about the great racetracks of America."

"Yes, places like Saratoga and Belmont, Gulfstream, Santa Anita, Arlington Park. The shrines of thoroughbred horse racing."

"You know what *I've* always wanted to do? I've always wanted to do a tour of the B-tracks of America."

"B-tracks? You mean like B-movies?"

"That's right. Places like Hoosier Park in Anderson, Indiana. Will Rogers Downs in Claremore, Oklahoma. The kinds of places where I cut my teeth."

Panther nods, considering. "We could do that. That might even be more interesting than doing the major tracks. If you wanted to come along, you could be my guide."

"What about the wife and kids?"

Panther looks at me strangely. "What wife and kids?"

"You know, the domestic situation. The trampoline in the yard, the above-ground pool, the golden retriever with the neckerchief."

He shakes his head. "You've got me all wrong, Mr. Harvey."

"Really?" I say. "I thought I had you pegged."

"You've got me all wrong. I was married once, for a while, but that's been over a long time. Water under the bridge."

"Kids?"

"Nope, no kids."

"What about your teaching? The Robert Frost Chair of Poetry."

Panther smiles and shakes his head. "That's the only hold-up, but we could leave as soon as the school year ends."

"When's that?"

"End of April."

I nod slowly. "You going anyway, even if I don't?"

"Yes, but it would be more fun with you along."

"Why? I insult you, I'm miserable most of the time, I drink too much, I'm a string of failures."

Panther shakes his head again. "No you're not. Look

what you did today."

"A moment of confusion. I forgot my place in the world."

"Wait a minute," Panther says, his eyes lighting up, "I've got an idea: we could *co*-write the book! You could write a preface for it, or we could write alternating chapters, or —"

"Or," I say, an idea taking shape where no ideas have taken shape for a long time, "you could write up the physical aspect of whichever track we're talking about — you know, the layout, the architecture, the atmosphere — and I could do the historical part, the track in its heyday, the great horses that ran there. Say we were at Louisiana Downs, for example, I could write something like, 'In June, 1986, at eleven years of age, gallant old Dave's Friend, winner of thirty-five races in seventy-five starts and earner of over a million dollars, finished a fading fourth in a low-end allowance, thus ending his career. "Unable to sustain bid," was the *Daily Racing Form*'s sad but succinct comment on the valiant gelding's effort.'"

"Wow!" Panther says, shaking his head. "And was that all true, what you just said about Dave's Friend?"

"Of course," I say, tapping my temple. "It's all up here."

"Well, what do you think? Will you come?"

"Yes," I say, "I will."

"You will?"

"Assuming I'm still alive," I add, "and assuming I don't change my mind."

I know what heaven will be like.

I'll be able to drink with impunity, never getting too

drunk, never getting sick or hungover.

I'll be able to smoke as much as I want and never be short of breath. Smoke a little dope, too, if I feel like it.

In heaven, Finn Boyle and I will go to Gents as often as we want and we'll never get kicked out, not even if Finn Boyle takes off *all* his clothes. Chantal will walk onto the stage, but she won't dance. She'll look up — clear-eyed — at me sitting in the balcony and recite her latest poem.

In heaven I'll bet a thousand dollars a race and never have to worry about winning or losing because my wallet will always be full.

In heaven, Northern Dancer will still be alive, and when I summon up the '64 Belmont Stakes, not only will I be there to watch it, but I'll be aboard. That's right, I'll be in the irons, hand-riding like a maniac, waving my whip in front of his right eye to keep him focused, and this time he'll win.

In heaven *all* the great horses will still be alive. Man o' War. Secretariat. Citation. And there'll be no horses with squished names.

All the great jazz musicians will be there, too. Charles Mingus, for starters. If I want to have a drink with Charles Mingus, I'll arrange it. If I want him to play some music for me, I'll conjure up a nightclub and I'll say, "Mr. Mingus, would you play 'C Jam Blues' for me?" and he'll do it. He'll even invite me to stand in, and lo and behold, there'll be a tenor saxophone in my hands — John Coltrane's sax. I'll look up, and Trane'll nod to me from the bar, as if to say, "Go ahead, talk to me" — and wonder of wonders, I'll play it brilliantly.

If I want to know anything about my life, all I'll have to do is ask. If I want to replay the happiest day of my life, I'll be able to. If I can't remember which day was the happiest, someone up there will be able to tell me and do the programming for me.

I'll find out the answers to all the big questions, of course — the extent of the universe, the meaning of life — but if I want to know mundane things, that information will be available, too — how many pairs of shoes did I go through, how many toothbrushes?

How many triactors did I win? How much money did I lose?

How many times did I sit at this stool and say, "Dexter, a Bushmills, please"?

I won't have to ask how many women I was with because I know the answer. I remember every one of them.

Even if they don't die before I do, Barbara and Sylvie will be there in heaven, waiting for me. They'll say, "Oh, Priam, you were so much trouble, but we love you anyway, we really do."

If I want to wear the hair shirt for a while, I'll be able to do that, too. How many lies did I tell? How many betrayals did I commit? How many friends did I lose? How many people, who at one time or another loved me, stopped loving me?

I don't think I'm going to want to wear the hair shirt too much. After all, heaven's supposed to be a happy place. It's supposed to be a place where a man can forget all the things that troubled him in the world.

There'll be no dog shit in heaven.

No houseflies.

No regret.

There'll be no perversity in heaven. In heaven, grown men won't molest children.

There'll be no torture in heaven.

No misery or heartbreak. My son will be alive in heaven, standing next to me, tall and handsome.

If I want to go back in time, I'll be able to do it. I'll be able to see the birth of Christ or Custer's Last Stand or Cleopatra's levee in the tub, her eunuchs waving their palm fronds over her. I'll be able to see what she looked like, and Shakespeare and Pocahontas and Catherine the Great and Christ.

But, as I say, the best thing about heaven concerns drinking. In heaven, Anna won't badger me. Instead she'll lie on her back on a fluffy white cloud, and she'll say, "Darling, pour yourself another one and come lie down beside me here and tell me all about jazz." And when I'm finished talking about jazz I'll ask her if she wants to make love, and she'll be happy to have me. *Happy* to have me.

Then I'll conjure up a sunny April morning and a beautiful ravine, and I'll walk down into the ravine and lean on the railing of a wooden bridge that crosses a narrow stream, and I'll light up a smoke and inhale, and it'll be deeply satisfying, like it used to be, and I'll stare down into the clean, clear, pure water — no tires or grocery carts in *this* stream — for as long as it suits me to do so.

ELEVENTH RACE

POST TIME: 5:50 P.M.

(1 MILE 70 YARDS.
3- AND 4-YEAR-OLD MAIDENS.
CLAIMING $10,000.
PURSE $16,200.)

1 FIELD HOLLER
2 ACOUSTIC GRILL
3 SMOKEGITSINYEREYES
4 CHOREOGRAPHY
5 NASTY LOOKIN'
6 FROG PRINCE
7 VIRGIL T.
8 BEACHBALL
9 TWELVE TREES
10 HOME BOY
11 UNION

I've got no business betting cheap maidens in November when their owners are telling their trainers to do whatever is necessary to win some money to tide them over the winter and add to that the fact that I've only got eight dollars to my name, but I still kind of like the nine-horse in here, Twelve Trees. He's a gelded son of Forestry out of a Two Punch mare named Twelve Rounds, so he's got some breeding. Maybe it's just a matter of time till he catches on to what it is he's supposed to be doing out there on the track. On the other hand, he's run seventeen times, it's not like he's a novice, and he's only been in the money three times, so I'm really breaking all my rules even thinking about him, but I don't know, there's something about him I like. I can't quite put my finger on it. Something about his name, maybe. Anyway, there's certainly nothing else in here worthy of note. Maybe Home Boy or Choreography, but they don't have much to recommend, either, except they look like they can get the distance, which nobody else in here seems capable of.

Dexter opens a bottle of Budweiser for me, and I make my way over to Dale.

"My man, Mr. Harvey," he greets me. "That was a brave act you performed. Foolish, but brave. You could have been seriously injured."

"I'm no stranger to serious injury," I tell him. "I've been seriously injured for a long time." I hand him the Budweiser.

"Thank you," he says, dipping his head. "I've said it before and I'll say it again: you're a gentleman."

I look towards the island. "Twins gone?"

"Home to count their shekels, I suspect. Plus, I think that little bit of drama over at the bar may have dampened their mood."

"And where did you get to when the constabulary were about?"

"Oh, I was around."

I nod. "I'd like to place a bet, if I may. I missed the tenth race entirely."

"Everyone did. We had to shut down till the dust settled, but the show must go on, as they say, and, as you can see, we're up and running again. Too bad about the feature, by the way. You deserved a better fate."

"I deserved a better ride — we all did — but oh well, it's only money. Put me down for eight dollars on the nine in the finale, please. On the nose."

Dale leans over to write down the information. "Duly noted. Eight to win on nine in eleven."

Zontar, who has appeared at my shoulder, says, "Dale, while you're at it, put me down for two dollars across on the three-horse, Smokegitsinyereyes."

Dale looks at me. "Another horse with a squished name."

"Yes," I say, "it's epidemic. Still, this horse has a squished name that's more or less poetic."

"This squished name is poetic?"

"Well, it's more poetic than a lot of squished names. Say it out loud and see for yourself."

"You know I don't like squished names any more than you do."

"Go ahead, say it out loud."

Dale makes a face, but he does it. "Smokegitsinyereyes," he says. Then, like a man who's always thought that he couldn't abide oysters, but who's pressed into giving them a try, he says it again. "Smokegitsinyereyes." He nods slowly. "Not bad, but I still don't trust it."

Zontar says, "I'm betting him because of the song. I love that song."

"Do you think it wise," I ask him, "to bet with your heart instead of your head?"

He isn't listening. "Jerome Kern wrote the music, I forget who wrote the lyrics. Irene Dunne sang it in the movie version of a Broadway musical called *Roberta*, but a lot of other artists covered it — Vic Damone, Boots Randolph,

Bryan Ferry, even an obscure British rock group called ...
don't tell me, I know this ... Blue Haze! That's it, Blue Haze.
But it was most famously recorded by —"

"The Platters," I say.

"That's right!" He beams at me. "I love that song. I'm
going to see if it's in the catalogue. I may just sing it tonight."

Zontar heads back to the bar, and I turn to Dale. "Have
you got a quarter you can lend me?"

"For you, Mr. Harvey, anything."

I walk over to the pay phone next to the doorway to the
lobby. I could have used the phone behind the cash register
and saved myself — or rather Dale — a quarter, but I want
a little privacy. I dial the number.

"Hello?"

At first I can't speak.

"Hello? Who's there?"

"It's me," I say finally. "Priam."

Now it's her turn to be silent.

"Just thought I'd give you a shout," I add lamely. "See
how you're doing."

"Well, I'm confused," she says. "I thought I was the
one who always called. I can't remember the last time you
called."

"If I'm catching you at a bad time —"

"Well, as a matter of fact, we're just going out the door."
She places her hand over the receiver, but I can still hear
her say, "I'll just be a minute, Jim. Be a dear and warm up
the car."

Jim is my replacement. He's tall, silver-haired, successful, a CEO of some description. The car, Barbara has told
me, is a Lexus, which he drives in the winter; in the summer he drives a vintage MG Midget and rides a brand-new

Harley Road King. Barbara was showing him a house and they fell in love.

"I'm sorry, I won't keep you. Just wanted to touch base."

"Is there anything wrong?"

"No, no. Things are good, as a matter of fact."

"How so?"

"Well, I'm going on a trip, for one thing. A road trip."

"Really? Where?"

"The States. Friend of mine and I are going to write a book about the B-tracks of America."

"Well, that's right up your alley."

"Also, I've been cutting down on my drinking and gambling. I know it's too late, really, to mean anything to you, but —"

"I'm really glad to hear that. You know I think the world of you. The problem has always been that you don't think very highly of yourself. You have to feel better about yourself if you're going to be happy, and the only way you can do that is by getting rid of your ... well, your bad habits. I've always told you that. Not that I ever needed to, because you've always known it yourself. You have so much to offer, Priam. So much to offer."

"Let's not get carried away."

"No, it's true. You should take one of those self-actualization courses. They advertise them on TV. It's all about empowerment. Developing the self-confidence you need to impress people with the fact that you're a person to be reckoned with, a person who's not only got ideas, but ethics, too. That's what they keep drilling into us at our realty seminars. 'The Three S's: Skill plus Sincerity equals Success.' Really, you should watch some of those self-help infomercials on TV."

Even when we were living together, Barbara and I had

radically different tastes where television was concerned. While she was watching infomercials in the bedroom, I was in the living room watching *COPS*.

"What else is happening? You said you were going on a trip, 'for one thing.' Are there other things?"

"I did a good deed today."

"What kind of good deed?"

"I saved a man's life."

"*Really?*"

"Yes, I ... uh ..."

"How? What happened?"

"A man was being attacked. I intervened, that's all."

"You inter*vened*? What do you mean? Where did this happen?"

"Oh, downtown. A mugging on the street."

"You weren't hurt, were you?"

"No, I'm fine."

"Priam, can you speak up a bit? There's so much noise in the background I can hardly hear you. Where are you, anyway? It sounds like a bar. You're not in a bar, are you?"

"No, no. The subway station. Just on my way home and I thought I'd give you a ring."

"Well, thanks for thinking of me. I'm really pleased about your news. About the trip and about your being a hero. You should get one of those framed certificates from the city. Did the police take your name?"

"No, the, um ... the police weren't involved. I handled it myself. The guy ran off, and I ... uh, I dusted the fellow off, and away he went."

"I get the impression you're not telling me the whole story."

"No, I —"

"Never mind. I'm just happy you're all right, and I'm very proud of you. But listen, I'd better hang up, we're supposed to be somewhere and we're running late."

"Okay, like I say, I just wanted to touch base. Oh, and one more thing: do you remember that time that friend of yours — I forget her name — let us use her cottage up in Muskoka?"

There's a silence on the other end of the phone, but then she says, "That was early days, but yes, I remember. Her name was Heather Simms. I haven't talked to her in ages. That was before you and I moved in together."

"We had a good time, as I recall. Played a lot of Scrabble."

"Yes, we had a wonderful time. That was during one of those periods when you had your drinking under control."

"One of those rare periods."

"You said it, not me."

"Do you happen to remember the name of the lake?"

"I think it was Rosseau."

"That's right. And if I'm not mistaken, the cottage had a name, too."

"Twelvetrees."

I nod into the phone. "That's what I thought. All one word, if I'm not mistaken."

"Yes, all one word. It was painted on a boulder at the shore. But why are you thinking about that?"

"I don't know. It just crossed my mind for some reason."

Another silence. "Well, I'd better get a move on. When are you leaving on your trip?"

"Next April."

"Oh. That's a long way off."

"That's all right. It'll get me through the winter. It'll give me something to look forward to."

We could start with Finger Lakes in Farmington, New York.

Then, let's see, Green Mountain Park in Pownal, Vermont.

Rockingham Park in Salem, New Hampshire.

Narragansett Park in Pawtucket, Rhode Island.

Suffolk Downs in Boston, Massachusetts.

Atlantic City Race Course in Mays Landing, New Jersey.

Penn National in Grantville, Pennsylvania.

Mountaineer Park in Chester, West Virginia. Charles Town in Charles Town. Wheeling Downs in Wheeling.

Then jump across to Turfway Park in Florence, Kentucky. Ellis Park in Henderson.

River Downs in Cincinnati, Ohio. Beulah Park in Grove City.

Hoosier Park in Anderson, Indiana.

Prairie Meadows in Altoona, Iowa.

Arapahoe Park in Aurora, Colorado.

Yavapai Downs in Prescott Valley, Arizona.

Ruidoso Downs in Ruidoso Downs, New Mexico.

Lone Star Park in Grand Prairie, Texas, and Sam Houston Park in Houston.

Will Rogers Downs in Claremore, Oklahoma. Blue Ribbon Downs in Sallisaw. Fair Meadows in Tulsa.

Oaklawn Park in Hot Springs, Arkansas.

Louisiana Downs in Bossier City, Louisiana. Delta Downs in Vinton. Evangeline Downs in Opelousas.

It's been a long time since I've thought about any of these tracks. A lot of them were probably shut down years ago. I don't know. I don't want to know. We'll find out when we get there.

I get back to the bar just as the men in the yellow jackets begin loading the horses into the gate for the last race. Because Twelve Trees is the only grey in a field of bays and chestnuts and because his jockey's wearing turquoise silks, I won't have any trouble following his progress. I look to the left of the screen for the odds. Fourteen to one. If he wins, he'll pay thirty bucks for two, so I'll collect a hundred and twenty simoleons, or thereabouts. Less Anna's fifty and the eight dollars for the bet and a tip for Dale, I'll still be up fifty-five or sixty. I rub my hands together. Suddenly, I feel pretty damned good. Better than I've felt in quite a while.

I take a look around.

On the stool to my right, Panther's asking Dexter for a Canadian.

Over at their table, Young and Arthur are still eating chicken wings. Young sees me and wriggles his fingers at me.

On the karaoke stage, Zontar grasps the microphone with both hands. "They asked me how I knew," he croons, "my true love was true ..."

On the stool to my left, Finn Boyle's chewing a long cigar.

"Where'd you get that?" I ask him.

He smiles around the cigar. "Young lady gave it to me. Young lady with a tight sweater and a cowboy hat. She helped me to my feet after the battle. Sort of a tight-sweatered, cigar-packing, cowboy-hat-wearing Florence Nightingale type. Name's not Florence Nightingale, though. Think she said Kelly Ann."

"Did you know that Florence Nightingale was a lifelong virgin? Died intacto."

Finn Boyle frowns. "I don't think Kelly Ann suffers from the same affliction."

"How's your drink? Need it freshened?"

Finn Boyle regards the tumbler in front of him. "No, I'm fine. I've still got most of a Duck Fart here."

"Dexter."

Dexter appears before me. "Yes, Mr. Harvey."

"A pint, please. Put it on my tab."

He steps towards the taps, then stops and leans towards me. "Thanks for what you did," he says.

"Don't mention it," I say.

Then Jessy's there, squeezing in front of Dexter. "Are you all right?" she says to me.

"Yes, I'm fine, thank you."

"I was worried sick about you."

"I thank you doubly."

She leans forward, right in my face. "But maybe," she whispers, "you shouldn't have any more to drink."

I look at her. "Jessy, considering what I've just been through, surely I deserve a drink."

"You know what I'm talking about," she murmurs. "You want to be in shape."

"I can handle a couple more. You're off at eight; it's not even six yet."

"I'm just saying. It's your funeral if you're not careful."

A bell rings as the gate springs open, and my eyes jump to TV #1. I pick up the grey immediately and watch the jockey angle him from the outside to the rail after the inside horses have sprinted for the lead. He settles in, content to gallop along in last place, which makes me a little nervous, but it's a long race, a mile and change, and his form shows he's not a horse with early foot. For the first quarter mile, he saves ground along the inside. The jockey's rating him nicely. Into the backstretch he starts to pick up horses and in no time he's tenth, then ninth, then eighth. For the moment, at least, he's got clear sailing along the rail. As the field heads into the far turn, he swings out to move between tiring horses and before I know it he's fifth, then fourth, then third, but the leaders, Acoustic Grill and Smokegitsinyereyes, are still a good eight lengths in front. They'd better run out of gas soon, because place and show are no good to me. As they straighten out at the top of the lane, the jockey whacks Twelve Trees left-handed on the hindquarters — twice, three times — and he *really* begins to roll. Midway down the stretch, he motors past Acoustic Grill and now there's only Smokegitsinyereyes to beat. Twelve Trees stays to the outside — he's a beautiful, long-striding dapple grey with an almost-white tail — and slowly, gradually, he's eating into the lead, he's at the other horse's bootstraps, and the jockey in his flashing turquoise silks is hand-riding like crazy. Seventy yards to go and he's at the leader's neck. The jockey whacks him twice more, left-handed, to keep his mind on business. Fifty yards to go and there's still a head between them, but we're gaining. Zontar's at my ear, yelling "Come on, three! Come on, three!"

"Come on, nine!" I counter. "Come on, you nine!" Down to the wire and they're stride for stride, nose to nose. I can't separate them. I can't choose between them. As they pass the finish line, the two jockeys stand up in their irons and smile at each other and shrug their shoulders. Even they can't tell who won. I'll just have to wait till the numbers come up, but I feel good about my chances. I feel very good about my chances.

Marquis Book Printing Inc.

Québec, Canada
2008